The Eye of the Clown

Alexander Crombie

TSL Publications

First published in Great Britain in 2022
By TSL Publications, Rickmansworth

Copyright © 2022 Alexander Crombie

ISBN: 978-1-915660-11-4

Cover courtesy of : https://unsplash.com/photos/YBzsJv3c1EQ

FOR MY CHILDREN

Acknowledgements

I would like to thank the following people for helping me to bring this work of fiction to fruition:--

David Miller, for his constant encouragement;

Anne Ridler for the line of poetry in Ralph;

Margaret Scott, for her perceptive reading of the manuscript;

My publisher, Anne Samson, for keeping faith with me;

The many of you, my readers, who have been kind enough to praise my earlier novel - you know who you all are; and, most of all -

My wife, Caroline, for putting up with my long absences at the keyboard.

Kate, 1969

It was the day after her life had changed for ever.

Restless, mechanical in movement, Kate roamed through the rambling house, rearranging a cushion here, retrieving an ornament there and instantly returning it to its place. Buried in her subconscious was the realisation that in time, soon perhaps, all this feverish activity would stop; that she might experience the release of tears, even collapse in on herself; but that time was yet to come.

Physically exhausted by the effort of clambering up to the attic and down again via numerous diversions to check on this photograph and that wall hanging, she finally told herself, "Kate, for heaven's sake, try to calm down. Make yourself a mug of your favourite mint tea. Try to relax." Indeed there was no reason why she should not do just that. The children she had managed to farm out to willing and sympathetic friends acquired at the school gates over the years; and as for Genevieve, well so far she had succeeded in keeping her mother at arm's length, answering her telephone calls curtly with garbled reasons why she should not just fly down from their old Peak District home to descend busily on the Weald and her only daughter.

Her tea revived Kate, vaguely comforting as it was in its familiar astringency. All at once she resolved it had to be done. The one room in their large detached Edwardian home into which she had yet to step was Blane's study, known to all as "Dad's Den," but now she had to break the habit of married life and venture in.

Pushing open the heavy oak wood door, Kate was greeted first by the cling of pipe tobacco, Three Nuns she thought it was called. Blane had smoked his Briar for as long as Kate could remember, though confining the activity strictly to The Den, particular about shielding the habit from the children. So redolent of the man himself, the smell, she thought, would linger on for as long as she remained in the house, a constant reminder of the past.

Kate crossed to her husband's desk under the window, pulling out the swivel chair, sitting gingerly. On the pavement outside the study window teenage voices materialised out of nowhere. Everyday insults were being cheerfully exchanged, and with half her mind Kate acknowledged that the world had to proceed as normal even while "normal" had forsaken her own little world.

The first object that drew Kate's eye was their wedding photograph, or one of them, dating back eighteen years. Taken outside the Parish Church in her home village of Hope, the portrait posed bride and groom in the centre of the picture, surrounded by guests and framed by an arch of ceremonial swords. Blane kitted out for the occasion in his officer's uniform, was caught full-face. With no hint of the weight-gain to come, he dominated the scene with the look of an athlete at the peak of his training. His expression was slightly quizzical, slightly humorous. Clutching her husband's arm, Kate, one classically sculpted cheekbone seen to best effect, was half turned towards Blane while reaching a hand up to control her veil. Lighting the whole of her face, Kate's smile was uninhibited.

Captured in time and space, the rest of the wedding party shone out in their own idiosyncratic ways. Closest to the newly-weds was Genevieve, a hand extended towards Kate's dress as if she had just spied a loose thread. More in the background Blane's parents stood together, arm in arm, composed expressions on each face. Bridesmaids were caught in mid-dance, looking around to see to whom their bouquets might be thrown; while Kate's brother Edward, Best Man to Blane, was arrested in the act of helping their ageing Rector through the lychgate, and dear Ralph, Blane's brother officer, half hidden behind a gravestone, his face alive with mischief, was in the act of drawing back his arm, confetti bomb precisely aimed.

Kate dragged her eyes away from the photograph in its gilt frame. Blane was dead. He had died some time yesterday - she was unsure as to the exact time because it had all been so much of a blur. At one moment her husband had been sat in their conservatory, scowling audibly at the pages of the *Financial Times*, and then heard animatedly on the telephone; at the next, he was collapsed on the floor, a thin thread of saliva tracking down from his open mouth.

Kate had been in the Rumpus Room at the other end of the house, bundling grown-out-of children's clothes ready for the church jumble sale. She would never know what instinct caused her to get up from her knees and return to the conservatory. Much later, with anguish in her heart, she would dwell on the turn of fate that had led her into teaching and away from her first love of nursing; but even so, would it have made the difference between life and death?

Consolingly, Doctor Price had thought not. In the days when people still spoke reverentially of the "Family Doctor," Price seemed to have something ageless about him. One of his favourite expressions was, "Well there we are, and where are we!" Yet this belied his skills and also his savvy as a general practitioner. Faced with what he was quickly able to certify as the death of his patient, Price had calmly swung into action with the aid of the telephone, which he found dangling from its cradle close to Blane's body. Practical arrangements made, he had boiled the kettle and sat down with Kate and her cup of tea. Though she was only half listening, Kate heard to her surprise that her husband had found it necessary to visit the doctor on several occasions over the previous months. One of these dates stuck in Price's memory as it happened to be the anniversary of the Kennedy shooting, so that the television news had headlined with pictures of Dallas and the book depository from where the fatal shots had been fired.

As Kate sipped distractedly at her tea, she listened as the doctor quietly and patiently explained that Blane indeed had been far from well. Of late he had put on a lot of weight and had not seemed willing or perhaps able to follow his doctor's repeated strictures around diet and exercise. Bleakly Kate thought of all those fried breakfasts followed by daylong pipe smoking with the smoke, she suspected, being inhaled. She also thought about the chance that had steered her husband away from a big corporation job on leaving HM Forces after Korea. A compulsory medical examination once a year might have made all the difference; instead Blane had set himself up as an author, and not a noticeably successful author at that.

Before seeing himself out of the house, Doctor Price asked whether there was any telephoning with which he might help. Kate said she would contact her mother when she felt up to it; but yes, please could he phone her friend Anna to tell her about Blane and ask her to pick up ten-year-old Jane and seven-year-old Jack from the school gate, take them back to her house and start the difficult business of breaking the news. Later, Kate said, she would go round with pyjamas and things, and start to feel her way towards comfort for the children, for herself.

....

On the third day with Jane and Jack again with their friends at Anna's house, Kate found herself back in Blane's Den. Her first visit had not lasted long. That portrait brimming with happiness and hope, had finally spooked Kate. But now she was determined to be strong, to search out whatever it was she should be looking for, not that Kate really knew what it was. The filing cabinet had a forbidding look to it, and besides which, it seemed to be locked. So she started on the desk.

The first drawers Kate came to appeared to be packed with accounts, statements of account from their family bank in Seven Oaks, some of them casually stashed still in envelopes. Gingerly she picked out one at random. It was dated three months earlier. To her horror she realised it was the first time she had ever seen a bank statement. In common with many another wife, she had been content to leave "Business" to her husband. This particular piece of business however disturbed Kate as there seemed to be a puzzling number of entries in red ink. Was there something bad about that, Kate vaguely wondered. But as she could not make head nor tail of her husband's bank account, she gave a huge sigh, hitched up the cuffs of her shirt, and moved on.

The next few drawers seemed to follow a pattern. The thread was Blane's writing. For minutes on end Kate studied the sprawl of long-hand, turning over the foolscap sheets with less than her full attention. Kate was proud that her husband was a published author; Yet she had found it hard to get close to his work, largely devoted to war and warriors as it was. Blane had always claimed that his literary endeavours brought them in reasonable amounts of cash; yet Kate had rarely seen hard evidence of this, while from time to time valuable antiques from both sides of the family had mysteriously disappeared without explanation of any sort.

Kate's reverie was abruptly disturbed by the shrilling of the telephone at her elbow. Reflexively she jerked up, forgetting that she was sat at a knee-hole style desk, painfully banging her thigh, and setting the mahogany rocking.

It was Genevieve on the phone. Breathless and rather plaintiff sounding, Kate's mother wanted to know when she could come down to Deering. Her case, she said, had been packed for the last two days. Deciding on the spot that there was no point in putting Genevieve off any longer, Kate assured her mother that the guest room was already made up. She was to telephone Kate in the morning when she got to the station and Kate would be waiting to meet her.

Replacing the phone, the first thing Kate saw was a small Yale key squatting on the carpet where the tumbled chair had been. Curious, she knelt down to examine the underside of the desk. There her groping fingers found a metal strip bracing the woodwork. A bit of experimenting and it was clear the key had been magnetically attached to the metal strip only to be dislodged when Kate had reacted to the ring of the telephone.

For a moment Kate stared at the innocent scrap of metal nestling in her palm, reminding herself of Alice examining a small bottle labelled "Drink me!" She took it over to the cabinet in the corner, slotted it into the lock housing and stood back as the top drawer swung open as if by invitation.

The drawer was virtually empty apart from a single concertina file which Kate fished out and took over to the desk. The file, she saw, contained just a couple of sheets closely packed with what she worked out were random headings with page references to books, books on the subject of war and warriors, some of which Kate thought she recognised. And yes, sure enough, there the books were, staring at her from the crowded shelf next the cabinet.

Obscurely disappointed, Kate returned the file, pushed the drawer shut and tried the second drawer. Stubbornly it refused to move an inch. Cursing silently, Kate was about to give up and retreat to the kitchen and a calming mug of mint tea, but remembered a little trick she had discovered with filing cabinets in her first job. She again opened the topmost drawer, then slammed it shut, simultaneously pulling at the next drawer down. The trick worked.

What greeted Kate in the second drawer were bundles of envelopes, each bundle tied together with pink ribbon. At a glance the brown envelopes looked as if they contained business stuff, yet on closer scrutiny she wasn't so sure, so she slipped the topmost item out of the bundle, taking it over to the desk.

Postage paid, the envelope was addressed to Blane in neat copperplate writing. It had evidently been sliced open with care. Sitting down, Kate was hesitating. Never in eighteen years of married life had she opened anything addressed to her husband; yet why should she hesitate now? Blane was dead. She drew a single sheet out of the envelope and read.

Darling Blanie,

Five days, five long days, and no word from you! Ought I to be worried?

Darling, you've always told me to be honest, so do you mind me saying, you really didn't look all that well when you left me. I found New Key's sea air invigorating, and bless you for the idea. I got rid of my Londonitis in the first few hours. As you may have noticed, our fish supper with that gorgeous Riesling put me in ever so good a mood!!

But what about you, Dear? You did look a bit peaky and somehow your colour wasn't right. On the road back around Stonehenge, if you remember, I thought I was going to have to take over the driving!

But please, you mustn't worry about Saturday night. You should know by now, it's enough to be with you, to be near you.

Talking of which, do say, when can we see each other next? I've checked at work and I've still got holiday due to me. Isn't it time for you to do a bit more field research for your latest book?

Anyway, ring me at our usual time if you can, and DO LOOK AFTER YOURSELF

I love you.

Mel

Anna

Anna Havers was the motherly type. One of the school mothers had once nicknamed her "Mother Earth Anna," and this had become commonplace amongst her circle of young or youngish mothers in the village and its surrounds. To all appearances she was a placid woman, in many ways Kate Farley's opposite. Yet Anna was known to be a good listener and collector of people's problems, spending hours at the school gate or on the telephone dripping sweet drops of reassurance into hungry ears. "Oh yes my dear, I do understand ..." was her oft overheard signature.

Apart from the children, Hughie, ten, and Rosena, seven, Anna's household comprised Nan's husband Paul, the family's beloved hound Hugo, and Maddie, their French au pair.

An insurance underwriter by profession, Paul Havers divided his day between the County Town where he had a small office, and his home where much time was spent fighting his wife for the phone, but where he had had a state-of-the-art fax machine installed. Paul, it had to be said, was essentially vain by nature, possessing an exaggerated opinion of his boyish good looks. He was what some people called a "social animal" with a sparky sense of fun; but at the same time he could be thought emotionally lazy and lacking any appetite for confrontation. Considered a "Man's Man," Paul was nevertheless happy to be friends with the whole world.

Maddie had arrived in the Havers' family when the children had been that much younger and more in need of her light touch skills. Meantime she had taken root while earning her keep helping Anna with the washing, cooking and ironing that Anna sometimes neglected. Maddie was French to the extent that she owned a French passport, spent chunks of time with her widowed father in Normandy, and in conversation launched into native French at the drop of a hat. That apart, she was as English as her mother, long since deceased. In looks, Maddie was a striking girl, who knew how to turn heads; but as well, she was amiable and easy going, and very much at home in the household.

In contrast to the Farleys, Blane and Kate, both of whose families were bred in the bone of the officer class with, it was imagined, inherited wealth to fall back upon, the Havers were, in the words of their detractors, "New Money." Leaving school early, Paul had started working life apprenticed to his father, selling shoes on Borough Market. In childhood, an indoor lavatory had been a novelty. One trading contact had led to another, and the machineries of finance entered his blood. Very soon he found that making money was simplicity itself as money had a handy way of making more money.

Anna had been born and raised in Norwich. Her father had spent his entire working life monitoring the machines of Colman's, makers of fine mustards, and they had lived two-up three-down in one of the company's terraced properties. Anna had trained as a children's nurse though she had been happy enough to give up a career in the workplace after swaying up against Paul on the London underground. As she often reminded herself, Anna adored her clever good looking husband who in turn, and when prompted, admitted to adoring his wife.

All of which was just as well, Kate believed, as really Paul and Anna had little in common apart from their modest beginnings. Anna liked to attend Family Eucharist at the parish church and to help with Sunday School; Paul was anti religion. Anna sought the company of children, her own and as many strays as wandered in; Paul found them noisy and irritating, which was one reason why he spent most of his time at home in his makeshift office. Anna would drop off to sleep in front of the television around nine o'clock of an evening; Paul at this time would be brewing a strong coffee and clicking into top gear.

So what, Kate and others sometimes wondered, was the glue that kept this marriage together, apart of course from the children? A possible clue occurred to Kate one afternoon when she had done Anna a favour by collecting Hughie and his sister from school and had stayed on for a coffee with her friend. Kate of course knew Maddie, often bumping into her at the school gate or in the village store, while in the Havers home she had witnessed the chemistry between Anna and the girl. It was part of Maddie's nature to be neat and nimble of movement, scurrying from room to room on helpful missions; but to this she added her personal touch, often throwing an arm around Anna, asking, "Now Dear, do you want me to start supper, or should I be helping Hughie with his French conversation?" Yes, Kate had thought, a definite chemistry.

Now Maddie was out in the garden with all four of the children, jollying Jane and her brother along with her own brand of sensitivity, a "*Ça va Cherie?*" to Jane, "*Mon pauvre petit homme,*" to her brother, gentle arms extended to each. A game of croquet she decided might serve as distraction, and Hughie and his sister played up to the idea, not knowing how else to approach their school friends in their dumbstruck state.

The children seemed to absorb themselves in the game. At a point at which the competition was getting hot, Jane accidentally flattened one of the hoops, bringing up a divot in the manicured lawn. Instinctively Hughie's arms flew up threatening protest but as quickly dropped to his side. He trotted over to Jane and together they repaired the damage, smoothing back the turf with slim hands overlapping.

Back indoors the children stood about, at a loss to know what to do next or what was expected of them in this strange new world. Anna fussed around, offering tentative suggestions; but again it was Maddie who took charge, coaxing the children to the television room to be joined by Hugo the hound.

The *Wombles of Wimbledon* was showing on the Box, and for a time the antics of Uncle Bulgaria and his fellow scavengers kept the world of pain at bay. Jane sat rigidly to attention, never taking her eyes from the television screen. Jack, thumb in mouth, divided the time between the Wombles and Hugo the hound.

Eventually though, with both children, the mask of concentration slipped. In Jack's case his mind strayed to the Meccano model that he and his dad had been constructing. It was a model of a mobile crane, but it was unfinished. Vaguely he wondered who he might get to help him put the final pieces in place. The really tough bit was the lorry's steering mechanism. Of course he had the instructions, yet these were not easy to follow on his own. One little memory came back with a small prick of pride. His dad had got stuck for a vital piece needed to support the elevation of the crane, and was casting around aimlessly among the unused parts. Jack had retrieved the box that the number seven set had come in. Reaching a hand down to the bottom of the box he had found the all-important piece - it was a flanged trunnion - and handed it to his father with a broad grin. His father's smile was the only reward Jack had needed.

For Jane, the memory, bitter-sweet in its intensity, was of a ritual long observed by Father and Daughter. The ritual concerned her father's appearance and choice of suiting. Whenever he or he and their mother together were going out to a Parents' Evening at the school, or something else like an anniversary dinner, Jane insisted Blane come on parade for his daughter's inspection. Sometimes it was only an imaginary speck of fluff that she found; yet her father never failed to play the game. Now, there would be no more parades.

Kate and Anna

Sat rigid at her husband's desk, Kate stared at the letter, stared until the script swam in front of her eyes. In contrast to the cold print of the envelope, the letter was a riot of loops and curlicues. As if the words were not sufficient on their own, the writer, it seemed, wanted to paint pictures, suggest innuendo. A lingering tang of honeysuckle drifted from the Basildon Bond.

Slowly, icily, anger took hold of Kate, her mind, her whole being. Three short days ago life had been normal. She had been going about her daily, her weekly, round, ferrying the children backwards and forwards, keeping remotely in touch with her mother, putting up bags for the next jumble sale, with no sense at all that her life was about to implode. Blane had been his usual silent grumpy self, but without a serious hint of health worries, high colour and occasional breathlessness apart. If anything the last few months had seen a slight but discernible lift in his image. He had started on a regime of a daily walk, and had actually bought himself some new clothes. Should Kate have been suspicious of changes to a man embarking on that dangerous region, Midlife?

Yet her thoughts in this direction were fleeting and confused. Uppermost was the burgeoning anger that threatened to take her over. Bastard! How could he do this to her! After everything they had been to each other! Abruptly Kate launched herself to her feet to pace around the house, fists bunched. And as she strode back and forth, unable to weep, the focus of her anger began by degrees to shift.

"Mel. Who the hell was this girl, this woman Mel?" She certainly didn't know any Mel; nor could Kate think of anyone amongst their circle of friends and acquaintances who might have caught her husband's eye. There was of course no address at the top of that letter; yet the letter had referred to telephoning, which meant, somewhere in the house, there must be a number ...

Back in the Den, Kate tracked down her husband's address book without much of a hunt. It was the first time for her to see the book, yet it did not at first sight appear to be other than straightforward. At a glance she recognised all of the addresses and telephone numbers she would have expected to find, family and friends in one section, business contacts in another. Nothing caught Kate's attention in the "Family & Friends" section of the book, so she turned to sift through Blane's business contacts.

Again she found a list of names, individuals and companies, that looked familiar, doctor, dentist, bank, publisher and so on. Only one entry, a phone number without an address, looked unfamiliar. This was a Flaxman Number, suggesting someone living in the Chelsea area of London. The entry read, "Chuck - Flaxman 2425." Finger poised on the entry, Kate thought. They had an American friend, Chester, known to his intimates as Chuck; but there was no way he would have a London number. Yet she mused, "Chester" rang some sort of a faint bell … Could it be a shortening of Chesterfield, or …" Kate worried at the puzzle. "Even …! It could be short for Granchester and a lead to their favourite Rupert Brooke, "… And is there honey still for tea?" "Honey," giving her "Melissa, or possibly Melanie," via the Greek - or was it Latin?

Kate didn't care at that moment about the derivation; she knew instinctively she was right. She didn't pause for a moment but picked up the phone and dialled the Flaxman number.

The call was answered on the third ring. An anxious and slightly breathless female voice announced, "This is Mel. Who is that, please?"

In those seven seconds something happened to Kate. It was like the first plunge of a lift cage; it had the shock effect every bit as electric as the discovery of her husband's body. The voice repeated, "Who is that, please?"

"I am Blane's wife."

The silence from the other end of the phone stretched out to fill the immensity of the moment. Kate was not about to break that silence. Thoughts were coming together. She was not going to burst in with "My husband's dead!" not straight away. She had to keep the upper hand, show this girl she was nothing more than a superfluous cog in the greater assembly of Kate's family history. This way she could keep control, even conjure revenge of some kind.

"Oh!" was all that followed the long intake of breath.

Another silence before Kate spoke again. "You ought to know that I've read your letters to my husband, so I know all about your sordid little affair. But I'm giving you the chance to deny it if you want to, if you can, if you dare."

Given the chance, Kate might have taken the last "if" back, because the girl at the other end of the line now reacted, and with spirit. "Hey! Excuse me, 'affair' yes, I won't deny that, but 'little' it is not, 'sordid' it is not."

"Oh well then, I suppose you're going to tell me it's something quite beautiful, something the two of you have been keeping secret so as not to embarrass the wife and kids! Is that about right?"

A big breath, and then Mel came back with, "I don't know whether you realise this but Blane has been unhappy for a long time now. He's a lovely and sensitive man as well as a gifted writer; don't you think he has the right ..."

Kate burst in, "Don't tell me what I already know, and don't you dare talk about right! Do you think it's right to attempt the break-up of a twenty-year marriage and threaten, poison the happiness of two innocent and beautiful children? Let me tell you Miss, what is right is that you get yourself on a fast boat to Antarctica or some other Godforsaken place, and forget all about us!"

Mel's next came over with a frustrating calm. "Yes, they are lovely children, Janie and Jack. I once caught a glimpse of them one day when Blane was dropping them off at their school. You must believe, I do not intend any harm to the children. I'm not a femme fatale, I don't come with horns either; in fact, I would like us all to meet, to talk ..."

"Ah! Well you see, that's not now going to be possible because my husband is dead. He died on Friday from a heart attack!" The phone crashed to its cradle. The line went dead.

....

"Who was it who broke the call?" Anna asked. The two women were in the master bedroom. Anna had come around to see what she might be able to help with and to offer a sympathetic ear. Frenziedly, Kate was combing through Blane's half of the wardrobe, chucking a suit, a blazer, a smoking-jacket on to the bed, scrunching shirts into a pile.

"I broke the call. I felt, well, if the wretched girl wanted to grieve, she could damn well do it in her own time without involving me. Cruel? I was feeling bloody cruel. I suppose I needed to hang on to my status as the wife, as the widow. I was determined I was not going to be histrionic so no talk about checking for transferred diseases. But do you know, Anna, it's silly, but it's the little things that trip you, that hurt the most, like the girl calling Jane Janie, Blane's own pet name for her."

"My dear, I do understand. I don't know how you could have handled it better." Anna was sat on the window seat, untangling a skein of purple wool.

Nearing the end of the wardrobe, Kate reached down her husband's old uniform in which he had been married. Gazing at it for a long moment, she decided it needed a clean. "I suppose it was me. I never understood his frailties. Perhaps his failings were greater than I ever realised." She hung the uniform on a better hanger and looked across the bed to her friend. "If I'd found out about the girl before Blane died then somehow it might have been easier. There could have been a chance ... a chance for him to say, 'Kate, you know don't you, it's really you that I love.'"

Anna looked up from her wool with a start. "Don't you dare blame yourself, Kate. I never did."

Kate came round from the bed to sit alongside Anna on the window seat. "What do you mean, 'You never did?'"

Anna dropped her handiwork into her lap and drew a deep breath. "I don't think anyone around here knows about this."

"About what?"

"As well as Girl Friday, resident linguist and stand-in mother, our Maddie is Paul's mistress. I am part of a *ménage-à-trois*."

Their eyes met in an honest gaze. A moment and, "You're right, I had no idea. You've always seemed, well, so normal."

Anna leaned again to her wool. "I know you're not going to spread it around, so I'll tell you. It was Christmas a couple of years back. Funny how Christmas has a habit of throwing up an unexpected crisis. We were all at Midnight Mass, first time for Hughie and Rosena." Anna turned to look out of the window, her gaze resting on a pair of sparrows engaged in their own little courtship ballet. "Paul was sitting between me and Maddie, the children in the pew in front. Between carols I leaned forward to tell the children to stop fidgeting. Out of the corner of my eye and despite the shadows of the candlelight, I clearly saw Maddie fold a square of paper and push it into Paul's pocket, his trousers' pocket. At the time I thought no more about it. If anything I thought it might be a joke for the home-made crackers we were yet to finish off for the big day."

"But then, later, you came across the note when hanging up your husband's best suit?" Kate realised she was slipping into the language of betrayal. "And the note said?"

"*Joyeux Noël! Je t'adore, Monsieur*, followed by a squiggle that might have been meant as a kiss. Even then, naive as I am, I didn't suspect they were lovers. Maddie had always been tactile, a bit flirtatious - with all of us, not Paul especially." Anna glanced again at the garden. Mr and Mrs Sparrow's courtship seemed to have run its course as there was now no sign of the couple. "I remember sitting down on our bed, our marital bed, heart racing, trying to digest, to rationalise my discovery. In some senses it seemed classic Mills and Boon - 'Much younger woman flatters susceptible male!' But then I got to asking myself the awful question, 'Do you, Maddie, feel sorry for him?'"

"So how did you deal with all this?" Kate asked.

"OK so I remembered something I'd once read in a novel, something like, 'The French manage things better; they keep their mistresses tucked away the other side of town.' But straight away I dismissed this as any sort of a solution. That way I would lose control, and Kate, if I knew anything I knew somehow I had to keep control of the situation. I needed Paul; the children needed their father as a daily presence in their lives. Don't laugh, but we even needed Maddie - where would we ever find a more resourceful au pair?"

"Which of them did you tackle first?"

"Oh naturally you would expect me to say Paul. Trouble was, I knew just how he would react, with bluster and denial. You see, warming to the dynamics of the thing I'd got into sleuth mode, found some grisly evidence, mostly in Maddie's room. So I decided to tackle the girl first, setting out with her to the shop, taking the long way round. I opened up with 'Now Maddie, you need to know, I've tumbled to the truth about you and Paul.' Well, as you might expect, she stopped dead in her tracks, looking around everywhere except at me. Fortunately we'd happened to stop right next that bench, you know, the one that overlooks the lake, so that I was able to pull her down and look her in the eye. Maddie had gone a whiter shade of pale by this time, but having started I had to go on. 'I suspect that my husband is most likely besotted, and if so there's nothing I can do about that.' The girl opened wide that big red mouth of hers as if to protest, but I charged on. 'What I don't want is for the two of you to be slinking off to grubby hotel rooms or, God help us, deserted hay lofts. I have to come out of this with some dignity. So I'm going to suggest that we keep as we are, that you continue to live with the family, carry on as au pair, but doing nothing to flaunt your affair in front of me, or anyone else. Above all, Maddie, the children should never know the truth, you understand?'"

"How did she take it?"

"I'm tempted to say, like a woman of the world. The colour rushed back to her face, a gentle hand was slipped into mine, and with her habit of mixing her languages she simply said, '*Absolument*, I understand.' At which we got up and went for the shopping with me left wondering which of us was the more worldly wise."

"And it's worked like that for the past two years?"

"Oh pretty much. Of course, it was a little harder to talk Paul round. As I'd expected, he blustered and evaded for a day or two, but then he fell into line, if a little sheepishly." The final tangle was thrust from the purple wool with a sigh of satisfaction. "Only trouble was, their routines didn't exactly fit with mine. Often I'd find I was dropping off in front of the television, waking up with a start and wondering whether it was the right time to join Paul in the marital bed or whether he'd still be with Maddie in her room. Once I remember all three of us overslept so that Hughie and Rosey had to forage for their breakfast before getting themselves off to school, Rosey wearing one white sock and one red sock."

Kate got up with a start. "Oh gosh and they'll soon be coming out. I'll have to hurry! Just tell me, Anna, does anyone else know about your, your arrangement?"

"Only Mum. She had to come to us for a week or so after Dad died. Her head was full of Dad as you'd expect; but that didn't prevent her noticing things. So I took her out for tea one day and in a quiet corner managed to explain the situation. It wasn't easy. Mum's indignant reaction was, 'Well, I've never trusted that Paul of yours, and now he's got it all on a plate! If it was me I'd throw the *madammoiselle* out tomorrow, bag and baggage! Send her packing back to France!' But of course I haven't."

Ralph

Ralph Ransom reached for the hand mirror the nurse had forgotten to take out with her, and for the first time he saw why he had nearly died.

Later, when it came to sleeping or trying to sleep, he had to remind himself who he was. He almost spoke the words aloud. "I am Ralph Kennedy Owen Ransom, son of Sir Hector and Lady Ransom of Tudors in the Royal County of Berkshire; born 12 May 1930; educated Winchester House, Eton College and Jesus College Oxford," the last of these following a spell of three years as one of her Majesty's Guards officers.

For the silver spoon had indeed been Ralph's inheritance, his brother and each of his three sisters being younger than Ralph. And being the son-and-heir, Ralph had grown up with something of the *droit du seigneur* hardwired into his personality.

At his Prep School this trait had come out in various forms. As well as flaunting the largest and best stocked tuck box in the school, Ralph found it easy to "Lord it about" in the words of his House Master, strolling everywhere, never running, topping off the pose with the help of his father's second-best swagger stick tucked nonchalantly under one arm. Focus for his younger admirers was the cricket field. Disdaining the mud and galumph of the football pitch with its native absence of style, he applied himself to shine at the beautiful game of cricket. Blessed with a natural eye for the game, Ralph broke all records with the bat, on one occasion witnessed by Sir Hector and the rest of the family, opening the batting and carrying his bat for a 120 runs. Lorded for the silkiness of his cover drives in particular, he was the toast of the whole school, and didn't mind that a bit.

Eton was to prove a natural progression. There was no escaping the fagging, the ancient institution of servitude to older boys still retained in most of the nation's public schools. In Ralph's case he was assigned to Blane Farley, though for the two of them the relationship smacked more of equal partners rather than slavery. Of course, he went through the motions, knowing what was expected, from keeping Farley's cadet uniform clean, to placing his bets; but when it came to fagging to the shops for cigarettes or Guinness, he found that Blane was always open-handed both with goodies and time to gossip.

As for lessons Ralph did just enough to get by, often handing in essays late with the excuse that he had been needed in the cricket nets. On one famous occasion he managed to smuggle himself aboard the bus taking the First Eleven to their annual fixture against Harrow, leaving Hancock Minor to stooge for him through Geography and double Latin. Of course he had been rumbled by authority, but not before he had grabbed the chance to stand in for an off-colour member of the team and score a match-winning tally of runs.

Leaving school aged seventeen with examination results verging on the respectable, Ralph passed up university, preferring instead to go for a commission in the army. Keen to follow in the footsteps of Blane Farley, he wanted to try for the Gloucesters. Dug in on the stony ridges of Korea, stubbornly resisting the massed onslaughts of the Chinese invader, the Gloucesters were making history; and it was from Korea Blane returned, not one but two wound stripes decorating his number one uniform. Sir Hector however had steered Ralph in the direction of his old regiment of Guards with the result that he had missed out on active service. Father Ransom, one of a long tradition of military men, had fought his way through the later stages of the Great War, winning the Military Cross and Bar through the rain-sodden weeks of Third Ypres, and wanted nothing more than to see his eldest son maintain the family tradition.

When not in barracks at Chelsea, Ralph spent much of his days dressed to the nines, sauntering Piccadilly or Pall Mall or The Haymarket like some latter day Beau Brummell, idly eyeing up the girls before dining at his club. Later on, Pall Mall would be exchanged for the King's Road, dress uniform for a rather rakish flying jacket. But whatever the guise, Ralph found the girls unerringly attracted by his clean-cut good looks, so that he was slow to warm to the prospect of Oxford and hard work. The need for a career loomed like an unwelcome itch.

When it eventually came to it, his arrival at Jesus College proved less of a bore than he had expected. With the three years of his commission behind him he was older than most of his contemporaries. This fact gave Ralph something of an air of worldliness, almost of superiority. Strolling around Carfax and The Turl following a leisurely breakfast, he would acknowledge the greetings of younger undergraduates with the merest nod. Of an evening he liked to hold court in the Mitre, arguing the case for Dostoevsky's anti-heroes or posing philosophical dilemmas to a circle of admiring acolytes.

Ralph indeed could have wished he was reading English or Russian or a host of modern languages appropriate to what he considered his temperament. As it was, he was entered on a beastly tough Law degree thanks to Sir Hector who was determined his son-and-heir should go on to qualify as a barrister. So Ralph put in an appearance at the minimum of lectures and tutorials, thus allowing him the time to devote to the OUDS and memorable productions such as The Cherry Orchard and Uncle Vanya.

Ralph came down from Oxford with a nominal degree thanks to an Igretat interview based on his assertion he had been suffering from Mumps during the final two papers. Now graduated and without his feet being allowed to touch the ground, he entered Barristers' Chambers in Lincoln's Inn where his Pupil Master turned out to be a contemporary and friend of Sir Hector. Ralph hated the regime for it proved far too much like hard work. All the same, he ate his dinners and perfected his court bow and generally did his best to ingratiate himself with those in power which included the Chief Clerk, especially the Chief Clerk. Despite himself the outcome had been full fledgling in the Law, lending Ralph a certain status when in due course he was a guest at Blane and Kate's nuptials, Kate for whom he nursed a lingering tenderness.

The years rolled by. Ralph gave up his practice at the Bar or perhaps the Bar gave him up, he was never quite sure which it was. In place of Lincoln's Inn and the South East Circuit, he obtained a post as a junior lecturer in a small department of a red-brick university, teaching Comparative Law and Politics in preference to English Land Law and Torts.

Suddenly so it seemed, cash was tight, credit ever harder to wangle. He was obliged to go down-market for his wheels. He almost wept when parting with the last of his sports models, taking in part-exchange a rather cranky and clapped out Land Rover.

Around this time Sir Hector died following a fall in the hunting field. Recovering from the shock of losing a parent, Ralph browsed briefly on the thought that he might now be coming into his estate, only to discover after the reading of his father's will that the estate was in fact mortgaged to the hilt. And as for the rest of the family, he found with a shock that he was now a stranger. His mother seemed to have retreated into her shell. She was still his mother, but she had become distant. Brother Philip, it seemed, eked out a living working in a second hand bookshop in the Charing Cross Road - or was it Frith Street - Ralph could never remember. Philip remained unmarried and Ralph vaguely thought he might "bat for the other side," as the saying then went. As for Ralph's sisters, each by now was smugly and comfortably married and busy producing his nephews and nieces. Ralph had tried without much enthusiasm to draw his brothers-in-law into conversation, but these attempts had led nowhere.

Ralph occupied a modest suite of rooms at the top of one of the halls of residence of the red-brick university. One evening when he was feeling particularly sorry for himself, he happened to catch a glimpse of his face in the bathroom mirror. It reminded him that he hadn't shaved that day. Obliged to face himself he decided for a chap of his age he still had what it took, looks-wise. There and then he resolved to do something about it. He had only once been out with one of his students, the practice being frowned upon by authority. On the other hand, there was that lively girl behind the bar at the Exeter who treated him to lingering looks whenever he breezed in for a pint of Worthingtons. Yes, Ralph decided, he would drive by and see if Rita - he thought she was Rita - might be up for a nightcap once she was off-duty. He took a hurried shower before changing into his best blazer and slacks.

Rita was indeed on duty; Rita was up for it, scrabbling for her coat as soon as the landlord called time. They drove out of town to a little old hostelry in the hills where horse brasses winked cheerily and law enforcement seldom checked on time-keeping. Ralph took it easy with drinks - he was driving after all - but this did not in any way detract from his enjoyment of his break-out and the company of Rita. He was framing the thought, "Do you I wonder live on your own, stroke, have an accommodating flat mate?" When the gong finally sounded, they reluctantly got up to leave their cocoon.

Later Ralph remembered that a thin film of ice had been forming on the windows of the Land Rover as they drove off. At the time he gave it little thought, still musing on whether he would be invited in for a coffee.

At the bottom of the hill he changed up a gear, heading back to town. Then, concentration lapsing, Ralph drove into the bend approaching the bridge. For a split second he looked over to the girl who had just come out with her most leading remark of the night, something to do with the snugness of her flat. Subconsciously he knew he was going too fast, but before he had time to correct they were charging the bridge. The tired old Rover hit the parapet at close to forty miles per hour.

A fountain of flame erupted, bursting through the rottenness of the floor. The world went white.

....

For days and nights on end, Ralph drifted in and out of consciousness. His one sensation was in his nose, in the whole of his head, the evil stench of burnt clothing, burnt flesh. From his bed he could see the porthole in the door. Sometimes he would catch the duty nurse peering through the porthole, the grim expression on her face signalling, "I've got to do this!"

As soon as he was able to take it in, Ralph learned that Rita had been thrown from the vehicle upon impact with the bridge, and had escaped serious injury, just one cracked rib and heavy bruising. Ralph himself had been lucky, if that was the right word. The following vehicle had contained not one but two off-duty nurses from the Intensive Care Unit of the County Hospital, who had managed to pull him from the blazing wreck of the Land Rover and beat back to a smoulder the flames engulfing his head and upper body. They had loaded him on to the back seat of their vehicle, one of them staying at the scene to care for Ralph's passenger and alert the emergency services while his companion drove Ralph the 20 miles to the City Hospital and its burns unit.

Now with a shudder that went through the whole of his body, Ralph replaced the hand mirror. The hands were one thing. He had got used to looking down at his hands. The face? The face was altogether another matter, which explained why his glance in the mirror had lasted for mere seconds and why, up to now, the nursing staff had been so careful to deny him anything to look into.

The face Ralph saw in those few seconds resembled nothing he had ever seen before. Gone completely was the handsome symmetry of the classic features, the full lips, dimpled chin and neatly laid-back ears, the profile that had turned so many heads over the years. In their place there had materialised a grotesque lumpiness, a livid patchwork stitching together grafts of new skin each of a slightly different tint.

That night and for nights to come, Ralph wept silent bitter tears, resolving that no one should come near him, none of his lecturer colleagues, certainly not his mother; for what he dreaded more than anything was the flinch, the look of pity he would see in their eyes. Dark and desolating images swam before his mind. The old soldier from the Great War who was still behind his collecting bowl outside Charing Cross Station, as the next great war loomed, with that face rearranged for all time by chlorine gas. As a small child Ralph had had nightmares in which the soldier had peered at him with evil in his eyes. Just how akin to each other were they, those hellish twins of evil and disfigurement?

From the first moment of his admission, Ralph had been placed under the care of a Mr Hendrie. Recognised as one of the top burns specialists in the country, Hendrie was a Scotsman. He had very still eyes, and cheeks never known to flex in mirth. When speaking he gave one the impression that he was taking each precise word out to look at it before utterance.

On the Monday of the third week Hendrie materialised at Ralph's bedside, this time without his customary phalanx of students. With studied care he placed a hand mirror at the foot of the bed before seating himself to stare for long seconds at his patient. Eventually he said, "Mr Ransom, I believe we can do something about that chin of yours. It will mean taking a relatively large flap of skin from your back. We'd be talking about a biggish operation, and I'm afraid I can't offer you any cast iron guarantees of success. We don't need to make a decision immediately. I would like you to think it over. At the end of the day, of course, the choice lies with you."

That night Ralph had a vision of an endless round of trips to the operating theatre on the top floor. Should he keep faith with his surgeon and bank the future on regaining, if not normal, an acceptable face; or should he simply get on with his life, aware for every minute of the day that his face was changed for ever? Either way, he had to accept that "Ralph Ransom and girls" was history; but what about society generally? Would it, could it cope with the stranger in its midst?

Ralph had not been bred, brought up, to cry in the dark watches of the night, but now the saltiness of his tears stung the crevices of cheek and chin. Would he be able to manage people's reactions, their double-takes, their efforts at sympathy? Or could he find a new way to project, a new form of communication relying on the eyes, his eyes, their eyes?

The choice as Hendrie had repeated, with measured finality, was his.

Mel

Mel Mulligan held the buzz of the dialling tone to her ear for seconds before banging the phone to its cradle. She felt numb, numb in her mind, numb in her body. After some time she staggered to her feet and sleep-walked to the bedroom, throwing herself on the bed and convulsing with hot tears of anger and shock. "How could he do this to her? How could he go and die?" It was so, so unfair!

Should she believe what the woman had just told her? Was Blane really dead, or was Kate inventing his death in order to destroy their beautiful thing? Grinding her teeth and thumping a fist on the bed, Mel resolved she must go down to Deering, confront the woman claiming to be Blane's widow.

Hours later, two gins later, Mel found her mind revolving. Yes of course, Blane was dead. Had Kate been inventing his death, surely she would have come out with it as soon as the call had connected. The woman had ended the call on her terms, no doubt to cut off the slightest opportunity for Mel to shriek out her first shout of grief. Grieving, was that something Mel should hug to herself, or was it something that had to be shared? And what of those poor children?

Abruptly Mel jumped from the bed, making for the bathroom where she dashed water on her face and risked a glance in the mirror. What she saw did nothing to restore the world to Mel. Her lovely auburn hair straggled in all directions; her eyes, perfectly round and grey, looked weird; the freckles on her cheeks stood out like alien crustaceans. Clearly she would have to get herself together. Food? No she certainly did not want food. Fresh air, exercise? They might help.

With the action of an automaton Mel dashed lipstick carelessly over her wide mouth before leaving the flat, forgetting to lock the door behind her. She made for the King's Road in the knowledge there would be crowds of people to distract her. For the same reason, she might go on to Hyde Park, back via Knightsbridge. As she walked, Blane's face kept coming in and out of focus. Was it already starting to blur, she wondered?

Reaching the corner of the park she came close to colliding with a woman who was scurrying head down in the direction of Pall Mall. The woman gave Mel a dirty look, before bustling away without breaking step. Mel realised that her lapse of concentration had been the glimpse she had had of a man cutting across her path who, for a split second, Mel had thought was Blane. The profile was uncannily the same; yet of course it wasn't Blane.

Trivial though the incident was, it took Mel back two years to their first meeting, for that too had been a chance colliding. Mel had got up from her table in the Lyons Corner House off Bedford Square and was half way out when a male voice called her back. "Don't forget your purse, young lady!" The voice had a smile in it so that Mel turned instantly on her heel.

"Upps! Wow! You've just saved my life, not to mention my mother's! Thank you."

Mel's saviour beckoned her to the spare seat at his table. "If I'm not being too nosy, how does your mother come in to it?"

Mel gathered her purse into her bag and looked across at the strong jaw, the twinkling eyes. "Oh, it's just that it's Mum's birthday at the weekend and I wanted to get her a Monet print, something she's hankered after for ages. But now I've just realised I've run out of time. Got to get back to my work, otherwise it's the chop for me!"

"Will you let me make a suggestion? I happen to know a little outfit on the Tottenham Court Road that's likely to have exactly what you're looking for. Will you let me try them out?"

"Oh but I'm sure you're busy. Please ..."

"Not too busy to help an attractive young lady, not to mention her mother. I've been up to town to do some research for my latest book at the British Museum, but I think I'm done for the day. My name by the way is Blane." He pulled a pair of paper napkins towards him. "Let's exchange phone numbers so I'll be able to report back on what I come across. As Mel left the Corner House a warm September breeze was kicking up leaves from the gutter, and the Fab Four from Liverpool were crooning "Michelle, ma belle" from the HMV records shop.

Blane had been as good as his word, phoning the same evening to report, "I have your print, and I think Mother is going to be delighted."

"But you don't know whether I'll be able to afford it," Mel protested.

"It's as good as yours. I've got it on appro. You see, I've done business with the place in the past, and the owner trusts me. If you want to tell me where you live, I can drop it off so you can see if you like it."

Mel loved the print which she found she could just about afford. They sealed their business over a coffee after which Blane went on his way with a courtly bow at the door of Mel's flat.

A week went by. Mel was in the shower when she heard the telephone trilling. Dripping all over the living room, Mel interrupted the trill, speaking breathlessly into the phone. "This is Mel. Who is this, please?"

"Sorry for making you run, but I just had to find out whether Mother liked her print? This is Blane, by the way."

"Oh, it's all right. I was just in the shower, but yes, Mum loved the Monet, thank you. It was so good of you to track it down for me."

A pause on the line, and then, "There's an exhibition of Impressionist Art starting next week at the National. I wondered, well I wondered whether you might be interested in coming with me to the preview? I know a bit about the subject, so you'll be in good hands."

....

Tyrol in late April. Mel and Blane took their coffees out to the terrace of the Heislerhof, the better to take in the magnificence of the landscape.

Snow still lingered in hollows and crevices and on the upper reaches of the mountains, while all around streams of melt water provided a constant soundscape. One mountain in particular - they christened it their "Friendly mountain" - dominated the middle distance. It was so real, so vital, it could have been carved from the blueness of the sky, and at certain times of the day they felt they could almost reach out and touch the craggy face. Completing the banquet of the senses a soft skein of wood smoke drifted towards the village, scenting the air with resinous pine.

"I know it's only our first day, but I'm afraid we've only got three more after today, so if you're okay with this I really think we should put our boots on and feel the benefit of a good long tramp." Blane sounded in robust mood.

"Yep fine. You know your way around these parts. What do you suggest?" Mel was so happy, she sounded as if she would agree to anything he might suggest.

"Okay, so I thought we might take a wander over to the Lottensee. Down by the lake there the Lottensee Hutte that does a marvellous Goulash so you won't need to eat again today! Oh and the wild flowers are an absolute riot at this time of year. Do you mind if I? ..." Blane bent to tuck Mel's trouser bottoms into her socks. The gesture reminded her of their first date. Leaving the gallery she had been unable to resist the ripe appeal of peaches at a pavement stall. High as she was, she crammed the fruit into her mouth with a gulp of delight, heedless of the juice running down over fingers and wrists. Conjuring a pristine and monogrammed handkerchief, Blane had come to the rescue while passersby looked on indulgently. Home again, Mel had set about the staining to her blouse and the stickiness still pervading hands and arms. This too Blane had been able to help with; so it had been no great surprise to either of them their progress had taken them to the bedroom by way of the shower.

Now they set off from the Heislerhof with vigour in their legs. The Alpine day sparkled, and Mel was in love with it all. "It's a rare thing I'm thinking, Mister!"

"I didn't know you had the Irish in you. You've kept that quiet."

Mel skipped level, attempting to keep in step. "Ah! well you see, there are lots of things you don't know about me."

"Try me."

"Well, for a start, my dear departed Da came over on the boat when he was nothing but a wee man. The family was from County Sligo on the west coast. All of his short life he was a frustrated actor. I could only have been 12 or 13 when he bribed me into learning the whole of Pegeen's part in *The Playboy of the Western World*."

"Can you still remember any of it?"

Mel took a breath while gazing up towards their friendly mountain. "'Aye, you should have had great people in your family I'm thinking, with the little small feet you have, and you with the kind of a quality name, the like of what you do find on the great powers and potentates of France and Spain.' Then Christy Mahon replies, 'We were great surely with wide and windy acres of rich Munster land!' Ah! My Da, the poor wee whore, he ever afterwards called me My Playgirl."

Blane let a little silence grow before asking, "So, your father died?"

"Of the demon drink. I lost him surely, I lost the only *Playboy of the Western World*, so I did. I was 15. I think Keelie got over it quicker than I did. They'd been drifting apart for years. You see, Mum is the practical one of the family, hugely focused on her career in the Rag Trade. She's a Senior Buyer. Dad? Dad was the dreamer, always waiting for the gold at the end of the rainbow."

They walked on in silence until Blane pointed off the path. "Talking of which, would you call those little beauties gold or yellow?"

With a squeal of delight Mel hopped and skipped to where Blane had pointed. "Oh Man! What are they called?"

Blane caught up, tucking an arm around Mel's waist. "They're Gentians. Aren't they just exquisite? They prove you don't have to go all the way to the end of the rainbow to find gold."

....

Mel turned into Hyde Park. On the banks of the Serpentine a young Asian boy was staggering around on stilts, a small crowd of his friends cheering him on. Mel thought, there was something of the natural clown about the lad. She had never been sure whether the essence of the true clown was humour or deep pathos. She couldn't help another reminder of Blane. At one moment he would be pulling funny faces to make her laugh; at the next, when he was unaware he was watched, his face would set, the eyes unfocused. This is how she remembered him as she had been with him the last, the final time. They had been struggling back along the Cornish coast path in the teeth of an on-shore breeze that felt more like a gale. Blane had pulled up to catch his breath. Looking far out to sea as if searching for America. Finally looking back he had said, "Dear Mel, whatever happens, promise me, you'll keep looking for that rainbow."

By the time Mel reached Speakers' Corner she had decided. She would go down to Deering.

The Funeral

Mel thought long and hard how to dress, how to present herself. What on earth was the right thing to do when confronting your lover's widow for the first time? There were no rules to go by. So finally she decided on her plainest dress, a quite sombre green tweed which, her mirror assured her, would look rather less than provocative. As for making up her face, Mel thought the washed-out look probably suited the occasion, so she did nothing about that apart from the merest application of blusher.

Mel took the commuter train through Swanley, getting off some stops further down the line, walking from the station in almost flat heels. The January day relieved only by a low sun, was bitingly cold so that she was glad of the enveloping donkey jacket picked out at the last minute.

As she neared the centre of the village Mel stopped in her tracks. The solemn tolling of the Minute Bell should have provided an early clue. Flocks of people, she now saw, were trooping into the church across from the pond. Of course, Mel realised with a start, this had to be Blane's funeral.

Mel's instinct was to rapidly turn tail. On this day of all days there would be absolutely no chance to see Kate on her own. A sliver of fellow feeling told her also that she would only be loading cruelty upon cruelty.

Then Mel checked herself. Blane was in her head now as much as he'd been since that fateful telephone call. Surely she had the right, the need to express her grief in this as much as other more personal ways. She waited until the last of the mourners had entered the church, and then slipped in, tucking herself away in a corner of the rearmost pew.

She was only just in time. Another minute and the double doors of the church rattled all the way back to admit the funeral procession led by Kate, the children and an older woman who could have been Kate's mother. To a bronchitic wheeze of organ music, the coffin appeared, all four bearers dressed in military uniform. Mel took in that a hat, presumably Blane's old regimental hat, adorned the lid of the coffin.

The organ wheezed into silence as the procession reached the head of the nave. The mourners took their seats; the bearers rested Blane's coffin and stood to attention; the vicar strode forward from the chancel, and the congregation was greeted.

The hymn Mel knew as "Bread of Heaven" was sung midst a splutter of coughing, and was followed by an obscure reading from the Old Testament. Another hymn, "Tell out my Soul," seemed to enliven the proceedings. Then followed the familiar reading from Paul's first of his letters to the people of Corinth. Mel tried to concentrate on the words, listening as if they were speaking to her alone. Vaguely, she took in that she was hearing a message of comfort, of hope for the future; yet when it came to "seeing through mirrors darkly," her understanding faltered, to be replaced by the face of her lover, and tender scenes from the recent past.

After a sequence of prayers, the vicar mounted to his pulpit, gazing for a long moment over the heads of the congregation. Many years into his curacy, he possessed the look and the tone of someone weary of the world. Unfortunately he also seemed to be suffering from a heavy cold so that, once or twice during the eulogy that followed, he was forced surreptitiously to wipe his nose on the underside of his cassock. All the same, the Reverend Arbuthnot launched into his address with a will.

"Dear People, I come before you today in the sight of God to call to mind Husband, Father, Friend, Blane Alexander Maxwell Farley, true family man, gallant soldier, dedicated Man of God."

Mel winced and dug the fingernails of one hand into the palm of the other. Pew by pew, handkerchiefs were being readied while ancient gas fires fizzed without disturbing the chill of the church.

Reverend Arbuthnot continued. "Blane was one of us. Born and raised in this village all too few years ago, he was quick to show us that instinct for leadership which was to mark him out for the rest of his life. As a young fellow, I am told, he loved nothing more than to take a group of his pals up to Bassett Pole, to the tunnel, where they would wait for the *Golden Arrow* to burst forth on its way to the continent. Always it was young Blane closest to the rail who announced the coming of the speeding monster.

"Blane Farley first attended the little private school right here in Deering, before going on to his Prep School, and ultimately to Eton College. At Eton our friend excelled both in the examination room and on the cricket field, and I could only wish that his dear parents were alive today to help us recapture his fine deeds with bat and with ball.

"Blane could well have gone on to distinguish himself at the varsity. Indeed I believe he was offered a place at one of Oxford's colleges of learning. In the event, as most of you will know, war intervened as it has intervened for so many of us throughout this century of sacrifice. Blane was commissioned into the Gloucestershire Regiment and taken to the other side of the world to fight for King and Country. There with his fellows he stood firm against those who would despoil their innocent neighbours. Sadly, Blane was wounded, not once but twice, returning home to us with emblems of gallantry on his breast. Only God can know just how far those wounds might have contributed ultimately to his passing from us."

A pause to allow water to be sipped in the pulpit and throats to be cleared in the congregation. "Decommissioned, our wounded soldier found himself back in what I believe is known as 'Civvy Street.' Eventually he set up as," a clearing of the throat from the pulpit, "an author, and I am sure many of you will have enjoyed, hmm, some of his hmm, publications. Soon enough Blane met and married our dear Kate, and in time they gave birth to, hmm, Jack and, hmm, Jack's sister.

"Now, I wish to tell you all that Blane and Kate were a most loving couple, nurtured in the sight of God and productive in their service to God's children. My hope always was that I would still remain your Pastor when the day came to celebrate twenty-five years of blameless matrimony with a blessing in this place. Most sadly that is not to be; yet it remains our profound consolation that our dearly beloved Brother is even now resting in the bountiful arms of the Redeemer. And so, we now commend his soul to The Almighty in the sure and certain knowledge of salvation."

Squeezed into her corner, Mel had ceased to listen some way into the eulogy. She felt desperately alone, and wished she could weep, shed her own private tears of loss. With an effort she straightened up. The congregation were again on their feet, singing, Mel suspected, the closing hymn. She had no intention of getting caught in the middle of departing mourners, so she grabbed at the chance to sneak away without being noticed. The burial, she knew, would follow next; she had no wish to be a part of it.

Outside, the sun was sinking fast. A spiteful burst of rain hit Mel in the face. The singing of the hymn followed her as she headed for the lychgate. As she entered the gate, out of the corner of her eye, she sighted a loan figure half hidden behind an upstanding tombstone. Motionless, the figure stood there staring at the door of the church. It was a man - Mel was certain of that - yet the figure was bundled up with clothes, the face hooded. Whoever the man might be, he was intent on seeing without being seen.

Kate and Mel

Something the girl had said during that phone call had roosted in the back of Kate's mind and refused to go away. What exactly was it she had said? Something like, "I don't know whether you realise it, but Blane has been unhappy for a long time now." She had also said something about not being a "femme fatale" and not having horns; but that, Kate had instantly dismissed. No, it was that one word "unhappy" that haunted Kate and kept on bubbling no matter how she tried to push it down.

Was it true? Had her husband been unhappy? If so, was she to blame? She knew she had never stopped loving Blane; but had that been enough, and had she still been "In Love" with her husband? Was it possible that Blane was the one, that Blane had somehow fallen out of love with her? Could it be that this young girl, this Mel, had somehow been the unwitting target - Kate would not entertain "victim" - of an early midlife crisis? The unspoken opposite of "He has been unhappy" was "I have brought him happiness;" so, apart from the obvious matter of age, what was that happiness that apparently she had denied her husband, only for it to be discovered with someone else? Reluctantly, Kate decided, she had to find out.

Kate chose a weekend. Her friend Anna did not hesitate about having Jane and Jack to stay. Phoning the Flaxman number was a spur of the moment thing, something not to be over-thought. What took much longer was deciding what to wear. Luckily a sudden burst into spring helped, so that the dress though not as daring as the in-fashion mini, finally chose itself, as did the perfume.

Riding to town on the Greenline electric train, Kate wondered whether she had been wise to meet at the girl's flat. A more neutral rendezvous might have been more sensible; but in the end curiosity had got the better of Kate and she had agreed to go to the flat in Chelsea.

The block comprising the girl's apartment had a down-at-heel face to the world, nearly but not quite seedy. Stood on the first floor landing, waiting for her ring to be answered, Kate mused, "Am I going to meet a predator, or merely a lost soul ill equipped to handle what she'd stumbled into?" In the event, Mel Mulligan turned out to be neither.

Mel greeted with, "Is it Kate? I'm so glad you've come. Please, please come in. As you'll see, it's not much, but it's home to me." She led the way to a box of a sitting room where Kate was offered what was clearly the best of the chairs. Glancing out the window, Kate caught a glimpse of the river, sullen surface ruffled by racing wavelets. "I was just making a brew. Will you join me?"

Fleetingly Kate thought, "If I was a man and she was a man I would refuse to sit down first so as not to give the other chap any sense of superiority. But we're not men, so we're far more sensible and practical than that." So she accepted the chair, drawing her knees tightly together like any young girl.

While Mel made the tea, Kate looked around her, trying but failing to picture her husband between the narrow walls of the apartment. Blane had been large of frame with a slight tendency towards clumsiness. Was it really possible he could have fitted the space?

Mel brought in the tea, and for the first time their hands brushed together. At the touch Kate felt a sudden shock, surely not of intimacy? Stiffening her spirit, she launched out with, "I have to tell you, when we spoke that time, the day after Blane died, I was so angry, I couldn't help but hate you." She was staring into Mel's lightly made-up face, taking in the profusion of freckles. "I hope you can understand that?"

Cradling her mug of tea, Mel went to perch on the arm of a battered old settee. She bowed her head. She had wanted, had needed this meeting, but now that it had come she found she was in awe of this elegant woman with her classic cheek bones and expensively styled hair. "Yes, of course I do. You had every right, I suppose."

"So then, how did it start? And did my husband own up to having a wife and family living half an hour away by electric train?" Her voice, Kate realised, had a strident, a classroom edge to it. Mel's voice was altogether softer, more musical, suggesting a laugh might bubble up at any moment, were the circumstances different.

Haltingly, Mel told the story of the Lyons Corner House and the Monet print, while leaving out the trivial detail of the peach, and the less trivial detail of what had followed. "To begin with I knew nothing about his wife, about you. It was not as if he wore a ring. Then later, quite a bit later, one evening when he was down and sounding full of soul, he came out with it. I think I may have spotted a child's toy sticking out of his briefcase, and I tackled him about it."

"Did my husband ever say in so many words that he was unhappy, unhappy with me or with me and the children?" Kate reached out to replace her teacup on a side table.

Finding the question difficult, and the forthright manner of its asking challenging, Mel looked away, took a big breath. "No, he didn't, I promise you, he didn't. He sometimes mentioned Janie or Jack, but he never once mentioned you or anything to do with your marriage ..."

"Then how ...?"

"How did I know Blane was unhappy? Simple really. I could see it in his eyes. It's possible," Mel paused, "well I suppose it's possible, that he felt he came second to you with your skill at home-making. Blane had had a glittering early life, 'Blane the Cricketer' and Blane the Army Officer wounded in action. After that life could have been a bit of an anticlimax. He believed in his writing while at the same time having to face the fact he was not that successful; and of course he worried constantly about money." Mel smoothed her dress over her knees, and looked into Kate's eyes. "But most of all he just needed to feel young again."

Silence stretched between the women. Eventually Kate said, "Yes, and it happened to be you who was there to rekindle the flame." Another silence. "Was it you I spotted at Blane's funeral?"

"Yes, I was there. I travelled down in the hope I might see you, to talk as we're talking now. I didn't know about the funeral. I hope you don't mind."

"I don't mind. I don't blame you. Maybe, had I walked into this flat today to be greeted by a photograph of the two of you, I might, well I might have walked straight out again, and this conversation will never have happened."

....

"Dear Anna,

Well here I am in Bridge of Allan - Bridge of Kate, I'm tempted to say - and reliving one half of my honeymoon. Jane and Jack are with their grandmother for the Half Term, and you, dear Anna, are owed a letter.

It must sound strange to you, but I've come up to Scotland to rediscover my husband. I may be sick of my own company by Friday, but I decided I just had to get it out of my system, and I do believe that distance helps you to see straighter. I may decide to drive out to Loch Catrine or one of the other stunning sights which Blane and I thrilled to 18 years ago, or I might just roost here in the hotel and stuff myself with their gourmet cooking.

I suppose what I really want to tell you is that I've met Mel. As you know, to begin with I was just so angry. All I could think of was "You little bitch! How the hell could you do this to me, to Jane and Jack, to the family?" That was why I reacted as I did over the phone when she suggested we should meet. You'll understand I hope, all I wanted to do was to grieve, grieve in my own way, in my own time. I wanted the girl to be and remain strictly one dimensional; I didn't want to have to picture long legs or winsome ways; above all, I didn't want to credit her with a mind, the sort of mind that could take over my husband.

This feeling, this instinct was backed up by social pressure in general and Genevieve and brother Edward in particular. Fair to say, Mother was outraged on my behalf, going on about how selfish men were capable of being, how selfish and also how childish. To her, marriage meant being trapped, having to stay put for the sake of the children, though I can't think that Daddy ever made her feel like that while he was alive. Had it been up to Mother, I would have plotted some sort of ghoulish revenge, tearing up and posting back their letters, at the very least.

In the event, and that long chat you and I had in the bedroom helped, I got round to asking myself questions, triggered by that old sore about the good wife being a lady in public and a tart in the bedroom. Was it that I'd gone months, even years without buying new lingerie? Was it that I'd stopped showing an interest in his writing? Was it simply that Blane and I had ceased to talk to each other apart from the day to day stuff about the children? or was it that we'd forgotten how to be tender, tender towards each other? You see, Anna, I was finding the emotional betrayal harder to deal with than the sexual betrayal. And I got to thinking about the way - is the word "pragmatic?" - in which you managed to deal with the Paul and Maddie situation. If you recall, I asked you, "Did you ever think about having an affair yourself?" and you said, "I wouldn't have known where to begin!"

By degrees I came to realise that marriage, even if it is fractured, still has a status, a value all of its own, at least if it has lasted for some time, thrilled occasionally to joy and fronted up to sorrows and hardships as one. That was certainly the case with Blane and me, and the joys and the sorrows would always be there and could not be rubbed out by some Mel-come-lately. You, Anna, you did it your way. You accepted that the man often gets away with murder; that it can be a case of bowing under the weight of an endlessly demanding child. You found your solution. As for me, well, I might yet find out that the widow is a better person than the wife.

But I was going to tell you, Mel and I have now met. I went up to town and confronted, no, had tea with the girl. I must say, I was all set to confront her, but somehow it didn't turn out like that. She wasn't aggressive, but nor was she defensive. Anna, she's just a pretty young girl who jumped into my husband's life by accident, and who was swept along by the adventure of the thing. I could almost say I liked her.

Anyway, you've had enough of me for one day! I'll see you at the school gate on Monday. By that time I will know whether or not I have found my husband again, or whether Bridge of Allan has dissolved into Brigodoon, illusion with nothing at the end of the rainbow.

Your Friend, Kate.

Edward

Kate's brother Edward, Edward Upchurch, was a year or so younger than his sister. A Chartered Accountant in a small town private practice, he was short, slight of figure, with a habit of ending sentences with "Quite so, quite so," a verbal tic which some people found mildly annoying. Comfortably into his thirties, he remained stubbornly unmarried despite Kate's unflagging attempts to match-make.

Edward was, had always been, close to his mother Genevieve who nurtured an overweening pride in her son's professional acumen and achievement. The single occasion on which she had lost her composure and found her instinct for family solidarity threatened, was when Kate had come up with a lame excuse for missing her brother's graduation ceremony. When Edward bought his first house, it was Genevieve who turned it into a home, choosing most of the soft furnishings and kitchenware, from candlewick bedspreads to china toast racks. In return, Edward frequently invited his mother to stay, collecting her in his stately Daimler from her home in the Peaks, and returning her again after what he termed a "jolly time."

Edward was a conscientious churchman. He liked nothing more than to debate finer points of creed and catechism with his local priest. While he was generous in matters of practical welfare, helping many an indigent widow with free financial advice, his largesse did not extend to parting with hard cash. "Neither a borrower nor a lender be", could well have been his epitaph. So Blane's visit had proved a trial for both men.

The meeting, the first between the two men in many months, took place at Edward's office in the marketplace of Edward's adopted home town, corralled in sober Georgian stone. Blane drove up to the appointment - for that was how Edward had styled their meeting - in his salmon-coloured Jaguar XK120. He was dressed formally for the occasion in suit and regimental cufflinks, and had even been to his barber for an overdue hair cut.

It started badly. Blane was kept kicking his heels in reception for over half an hour while the office bustled around him. Finally admitted to Edward's inner sanctum, not by Edward but by a girl who could have been the office junior, he found a distinctly frosty welcome awaiting him. Making up for his natural lack of inches, Edward sat, as if enthroned, on an elevated executive chair. Worst of all in Blane's book of etiquette, his brother-in-law chose not to get to his feet, merely stretching a limp hand across the broad desk.

"Edward old chap, I trust you're well? Thank you for seeing me." Blane paused, but in the absence of any response, pushed on with, "The first thing I've got to say is, Kate doesn't know that I'm here." A silence stretched between the two men. "Of course I know she'd have wished me to send you her love."

After a quick glance at his watch, Edward finally broke in with, "You said something over the phone about needing money."

Blane cleared his throat. "Yes, well, please understand, Edward, it's only a temporary thing. Hmm. Cash-flow I think you call it."

"Right. Have you brought a business plan with you? Ah no, I'm forgetting, you're a writer, are you not?"

"Well you see, my last book, you know, the one about the Seven Year War, sold pretty damned well. Result, I was hoping for a healthy advance from the publishers on my next book, hoping for something in four figures actually. However, it now seems the industry as a whole is going through a bit of a thin time ..."

"What have they offered you?"

"Just five hundred pounds, I'm afraid."

Edward leaned back, putting fingertips together in a studied pose. "So, you're asking me to lend you the difference, the difference between five hundred pounds and, what are we saying, a thousand?"

"Well do you see, it would get me out of a hole, and naturally I'd be repaying it just as soon as the new book starts selling."

"What's the new book about?"

"It's about Wellington and the Peninsular War. I'm ..."

"How far have you got with it?"

"Actually I'm still at the research stage, but ..."

"So, this loan, were there to be one, is likely to be, shall we say, open-ended?"

"I'd pay you interest, naturally."

"Naturally."

Another silence painfully ticked by before Edward, eyes on the ceiling, resumed. "Have you considered selling that gas-guzzling Jag of yours, getting something more manageable? After all, you must owe it to Kate and my niece and nephew to live within your means, wouldn't you say?"

Fatally mention of Kate forced Blane's mind to wander. He knew very well that Kate and her brother had once been close. One time, two glasses of Merlot into a relaxed evening on honeymoon she had let slip that as children she and Edward had enjoyed dressing up, Edward favouring girls' clothes. "Let's just be sisters!" had apparently been Edward's excuse. Now on his metal his pride stung, Blane reacted. "Don't you think I know that! I'll have you know Kate wants for nothing. As for the children, I fully intend Jack will follow me to Eton, and Janie, well Janie's a bright girl, she's sure to pass for the Grammar School."

"Eton eh?" A hint of a sneer had crept into Edward's voice. "Well you're certainly going to need something behind you if that comes to pass. You'll find you're spending a fortune on cricketing gear apart from anything else. Methinks old Wellington will need to deliver big-time. By the way, there must have been a hundred books written about his Spanish campaign, surely?"

Another silence. "It doesn't sound as if you're going to be able to help me."

Edward pulled open a drawer, rummaged and came up with a glossy folder which he handed across the desk. "Here you go. These chaps are usually good for an unsecured loan - I assume the house is already mortgaged up to the hilt. But remember, play by their rules. Any late payment of interest and they'll be down on you like the proverbial ton of bricks. The last thing I want to see is Kate embarrassed."

....

Ten days after his trip to see his brother-in-law, Blane knocked on Mel's door with a boyish grin on his face and longing in the rest of his body.

"Now then Mister, surely to goodness you're not going to tell this wee girl you've come up on the Pools?"

They bounced down on the old sofa, eyes bright, holding each other. "The Pools no, but fair to say, Playgirl, we are in the money!"

"Tell me tell me!"

"Oh don't worry about that - it's only money. But it does mean I can afford to whisk you off to, shall we make it Paris? Paris always used to be the lure for ambitious authors. Would you like to be transported to the Left Bank, live on love and onion soup?"

For five seconds she held him at arm's length, putting on a serious face. Then she said, "No."

Momentarily crestfallen Blane puckered his forehead. "No?"

"No, absolutely not. I can't stand onion soup!"

One second and then, man and girl as one erupted in helpless hysterics. They were laughing still as Blane scooped Mel up and bore her through to the bedroom.

Some time later, as their friendly patch of sunlight slid away from the bed head, Mel stretched out with a satisfied sigh. "*Alors Monsieur, parlez vous Français?*"

"*Mais oui, Madammoiselle*, though I was once told I spoke *comme une vache espagnol*. Any case I suspect it's not half as good as your Irish!"

She stuck her tongue out in a feigned gesture of vulgarity. "So Mister, that's enough about my funny old genes, if you don't mind. I'm not sure I'll ever get over losing himself, the best Playboy never to tread the boards of the Abbey. And it's not something I've ever been able to talk to Mum about. At the heart of it I think Mum was jealous of our closeness, the Playboy and me. She was always so wrapped up in her precious career, she had no time to understand the nature of the thing, the Dad and Daughter thing. I've even wondered whether my being born was a bit of an inconvenience to her."

"Hey hey! I'm sure that's not true?"

"I do know she resented the idea we were ganging up against her. She'd arrive home of an evening whacked out by work, to find the two of us tucked away in the study, laughing our heads off about some Soap the Boyo was wanting to audition for. I probably hadn't looked at my homework, neither of us had given a thought to supper. Mum would throw her case down, storm into the kitchen, and throw out something like, 'You couldn't even peel a bloody onion, could you?' Then of course there was the little matter of the Vodka. Dad cared rather less for Mum's cooking than for his staples of life, cigarettes and Vodka. Result, seven o'clock of an evening was the time to light the touch paper and stand well back. Usually I timed it so that I escaped to the bedroom before the balloon went up. Then later Dad would come knocking softly on the bedroom door, offering to dry my tears, promising that 'Tomorrow Playgirl we'll just have to start rehearsals a bit earlier, won't we?' Then he died."

Ralph Emerging

Ralph Ransom had made his decision, chosen his pathway to the future. In some way the choice had been made for him. After three weeks in hospital, having got used to the wary half glances of the young nurses, Ralph found one day that a new face was at the end of his bed, looking him squarely in the eyes.

"I'm Deaconess Hunter, and I've come to see you, Mr Ransom."

Taken aback that someone would voluntarily wish to see him, Ralph for the moment was lost for words. Miss Hunter - there was no sign of a ring - continued to look steadily into his face. Possibly thirty, she was hard to put an age to. She wore a rather severe looking suit over a plain white blouse adorned simply with a miniature cross at the high neck. Her face, completely bare of makeup, was round and restful. "I should explain, I am a Lay Minister and a street pastor here in the city, but I am also relief Almoner for this and one other hospital. It's my job to ease your path to being discharged, liaise with your family, your employers and so forth." Still holding Ralph's gaze, Miss Hunter went on in her soft uninflected voice. "I see from your medical notes that you have been given the choice, to undergo further surgery or to be discharged?"

Ralph lay back in the protection of his hospital bed and considered his visitor for a moment. "Deaconess Hunter is a bit of a mouthful. Do you have another name?"

The Almoner thought about the question, not used to being asked for her given name. She had heard that in the future name badges would be the thing, but that time was yet to come. "Cerys. My name is Cerys."

"Well then Cerys, I have decided. I have no wish to prolong my stay here or to be treated as a guinea pig. I'm content that Hendrie and his team have done a passable job with the patching up. That's fine, but I'm not interested in being fodder for articles in the medical journals."

"You are saying you are prepared to live a new life, a life that will demand different forms of self expression?"

"Yes, Cerys, that is what I'm saying. I've still got my eyes, thank God."

"So Mr Ransom, Ralph, may I ask you, have you been able to think through the transition, the process by which you will return, hmm, to normal living? I cannot pretend that you will find it easy. It is quite possible you will need help." For the first time she broke her gaze, looking down to her spiral notebook. "Let me see. Yes, you seem to be well off for relations," she indicated a pile of Get-Well cards strewn across the locker, "and your employer, the university, they say they have granted you extended leave of absence on full pay. Yes?"

"Yep, uni's been good, more generous than might have been. As for relations, I'm not bothered about seeing them, and I'm sure they're not bothered about seeing me. One look at my face and dear Mother is likely to run for the hills. My sisters are all too busy having babies, and my brother, well, he and I have never had much in common. He's been semi-detached from the family for years. He might not even know about the accident."

"Is there no one who you feel close to, someone who cares, a male friend, or, hmm, a girlfriend perhaps?"

Ralph shifted in the bed, seeking relief for his burnt arm. "I'm afraid, Cerys, you're talking to someone who's led a rather independent, a rather selfish life till now. For years I cherished a thing for a girl - her name was Kate. But Kate was spoken for by one of my old chums, and they've been happily married ever since, couple of cracking kids to show for it too. Can't think I've bothered too much about relationships since then."

"So, when you walk out the front door of this hospital, where are you going to go?"

"Always the practical one, ain't you? Okay, so I mentioned Kate. Kate has a brother who lives not far from Leicester. I happen to know that Edward has recently bought himself a house, a house that's far too big for him on his own. I'm going to land on Edward, take my time to plan the next move. Happy with that, Miss Almoner?"

The Almoner got to her feet. "This is my card, should you need anything I might be able to help with. Oh, and by the way, do you realise there's a letter addressed to you, here on the side? Post-marked several days since. Labelled 'Private & Confidential.' Looks official. I really think you should open it."

....

Ralph and Edward had met over the years, typically at child baptisms and Christmas gatherings. On these occasions the two men tended to get together in corners to debate issues of politics and religion. One such debate had concerned the student Raskolnikof. Edward had been adamant that

Dostoevsky's anti-hero was utterly nonredeemable, while Ralph had pressed the opposite case. Finally, sick of proximity to Edward's cloying aftershave, Ralph had broken away, keen to chat up the tasty looking girl serving the canapes.

Now Edward took one hard look at Ralph's face and was clearly not for taking a second look, despite the partial mask with which Ralph had left hospital. This apart, Ralph found he was being treated to a better welcome than he might have expected. Edward was solicitous in many small ways. He was intuitive and practical as he was with most of the lame dogs of his acquaintance.

For his part, Ralph relished the quiet of the house through the long hours when his host was at work, while even the quarterly chimes of the Town Hall clock provided a sort of reassurance. He knew very well he was floating in a bubble of time; it mattered not. For the time being, all he wanted, all he needed were endless games of Patience, punctuated by the study of giant jigsaws of Elizabethan London. Discord between the men happened only when Ralph gruffly turned down Edward's invitation to join him at church for Evensong which Edward assured him was but sparsely attended.

Some three weeks into Ralph's sojourn, Edward detained him at the breakfast table to air an idea. It transpired that of his many clients, one was a particular source of pride to Edward. That client was the county Blind Society, founded in the middle of the nineteenth century and one of the biggest charities in the English Midlands.

As well as providing rehabilitation and mobility services and aids to blind and partially-sighted people living within its catchment, the Royal Wycliffe Society ran a workshop employing some two dozen men and women, including war-blinded, to produce a range of boxes and baskets. Edward happened to know that the Workshop was looking for a sighted volunteer to replace their recently retired gofer. Might Ralph be interested?

Slowly, deliberately Ralph replaced his coffee cup on its saucer. "I really don't know if I'm ready."

"Quite so, quite so. Yep, understood. But look here Old Man, you've got to break out sometime, can't be cocooned here for ever, and it'll be an easy half hour's journey by train. Why don't you give it a go? You've nothing to lose. Take your mask if you'll feel better."

Ralph started on the Tuesday following the Bank Holiday. Briefed by Don, the Workshop manager, Ralph found the job was far from exacting. It involved him in minding the machines whenever individual workers went for their breaks; passing along messages whenever maintenance was called for; and going round with the broom to sweep away off-cuts and other detritus from around the shop floor. The routine was mindless, yet in a way it was therapeutic, and most of all he was not obliged to socialise with anyone or risk being stared at. If he thought about anything on his mechanical round it was to reflect with admiration on the dexterity and economy of movement of the Blind workers at their lathes. Just occasionally one might ask, "Who are you? Haven't seen you before," a question that puzzled Ralph until discovering that the Blind use references to "seeing" even if only figuratively. So a pattern emerged, and Edward decided he had done the right thing by nudging his guest into the light.

One day Ralph returned from the city to find Edward in quizzical mood. "Old chap, I've just been doing a bit of a tidy-up - you really are a messy house-mate you know." Edward flourished an envelope in one hand while laying the table for dinner with the other. "Found this laying around your room. You really ought to open it, you know."

Ralph sighed and reached for the nagging item, slitting it open, reading. A second read and the letter was flicked across the table to Edward. Edward sat down at the table and read the formal communication that followed the printed heading.

Dear Sir,
Re: Road Traffic Accident / Personal Injury.
As Insurers for the above Council we are writing to you to invite you, through your solicitors should you wish, to contact our office with regard to the accident in which you were involved on the tenth of February this year, and in which, we understand, you suffered personal injury.

This matter has been referred to us following issues raised by the Police as to the responsibility of the County Council's Highways Department.

Having exchanged correspondence with the Police and with the Council, we are currently continuing our enquiries as to whether the cause of the accident was the presence on the highway of a road sign, property of the Council, which may have been dislodged from the verge, thus creating a hazard to road users. The sign in question featured warning of the bend ahead of the bridge with which your Rover vehicle was in collision.

In view of our ongoing enquiries, on behalf of our Insured, we are not in a position at this time to make any admission as to liability. However, in view of the possible severity of your injuries we are putting you on notice by this letter that our Underwriters will require evidence of your medical condition and prognosis, and may require specialist opinion as to the efficacy of future surgery, dependant on the acceptance of any claim by you.

Accordingly, should you wish to respond to this correspondence, we ask please that you commence by providing identification or by instructing solicitors to represent your interests.

Yours faithfully and Without Prejudice ...

Edward placed a pencilled asterisk against the signature before looking up. "Well, well, well. This seems to answer some of the questions I've been waiting to ask you once you felt up to it. From the little you've said up to now, I'd been thinking the accident was entirely your fault, that you'd have been expecting to be prosecuted by the police for driving without due care and attention, in which case the more relevant claim for personal injury compensation would have belonged to the young lady you were with. This letter puts a different complexion on things. Don't please say anything to me or to anyone else about the accident other than, 'Yes, I remember hitting an obstruction in the road.'"

"Honestly Edward, I don't remember seeing anything ..."

"But?"

"I do remember a bump, a bump just before I lost control and charged into the bridge. If I thought anything about it afterwards I probably imagined it was a badger or a rabbit."

"Quite so. Now, what about this phrase in the letter, 'Efficacy of future surgery'?"

"What about it?"

Edward squared the knives and forks in their settings with symmetrical care. "Well surely you realise you could be in for a substantial settlement here? I'm talking damages for negligent care of the highway."

"So what has 'Future surgery' got to do with it?"

"Are we being a tiny bit dense here? If the specialist's report states that a further operation would restore your boyish good looks, that could influence the quantum, that is, the amount of your compensation, do you see?"

Ralph abruptly got to his feet, turning for the stairs. "I was given the choice. I chose to stay with my face."

A Bailiff at the Door

Blane, Ralph's friend and mentor, had died. Apparently he had died of a heart attack, suddenly and without any warning. Ralph's first thought was for Kate. He had never fully been able to suppress his feelings towards the woman, or rather the girl to whom he had felt so close back in his Eton days, fuelled perhaps by her admiration for his cricketing triumphs. Now he could only think back to Kate's wedding and the wistfulness with which he had thrown that confetti.

Edward, for his part, took the news of his brother-in-law's death very badly. It was not long since Blane had paid him that visit, hoping for a cash hand-out. Edward was sure he had done the right thing about that. Give an inch and the waster would have been back for more, and then more. It was not for nothing that Edward lived his life according to precedent. Now he had to decide how best to be supportive to his beloved sister, to Jane and to Jack; he also had the problem of Ralph, who was yet to tell Kate about his accident.

....

In the event the two men had driven together to the funeral. During the journey south, Edward became aware of a growing tension in his companion. Ralph had been quiet over the first fifty miles; now he was silent. Although he had brought his mask, he was dreading being any part of the gathering, dreaded most of all being the cause of deflecting Kate's grieving and her status and dignity as Chief Mourner. "Look here Old Chap, if you're getting windy, you're welcome to stay in the car. I can park up round the corner from the church, and no one will be the wiser."

They parked the Daimler as Edward had suggested, and Edward headed off for the church, whistling tunelessly under his breath. For several minutes Ralph sat numb. Then something made him stir and ask himself, "Is this really how you intend to live the rest of your life, Ransom? Surely this is the test, the first test, the reason for refusing further bouts under the surgeon's knife?" Judging the time to be right, aided by the distant strains of organ music, he got out of the car and let the music take him to the churchyard. But at that point Ralph's courage ran out. Rather than follow his friend's coffin into the church, he selected a large upstanding tombstone behind which he could see without being seen. From his hiding place he followed the service after a fashion thanks to the cues provided by the organ. He focused his mind on Kate, picturing her and the children sat solemnly in the foremost pew. As finally the doors of the church scraped open he levered away from his stone-cold shield and was in the act of breaking cover when he spotted a young woman hurrying for the lychgate. Momentarily Ralph wondered who the girl might be; yet his situation demanded action. He fled.

....

Returning to the Daimler, Edward explained he had managed a quiet word with Kate, including a few stark details of Ralph's changed appearance. He had asked his sister, would she prefer that he drove Ralph back up the motorway, or would she want to see Ralph at home after the wake. Kate had told her brother she had been hoping that Ralph would be at Blane's funeral, and that of course he must come to the house.

Edward borrowed Kate's house keys and drove Ralph the short distance to the house. There Ralph was to lie low for the two hours or so that sister and brother would be occupied with the wake, the venue for which was the village pub. So it was that Ralph was left restlessly to roam the house in which so many joyous events had been celebrated down the years.

By chance the first thing that drew his eye was a photograph of Kate and Blane's wedding. It was not hung in pride of place on the wall, but rested incongruously on a kitchen work-top, alongside a cleaning rag. Evidently, Ralph decided, Kate had been in the act of sprucing it up when she had run out of time.

Ralph studied the photograph. Of course he had seen it before, but without ever really seeing it. Eighteen years had passed, and yet the dynamic of the portrait held true - with the one obvious exception. Although he had put on a lot of weight over the intervening years, Blane had remained the Blane of the photograph, humorous twinkle and all. Kate? Well Kate was Kate, with the sort of fine-featured face that would never fully age. And her love for her newly-minted husband shone out to the world. Edward, lending his arm to the clergyman, was alerting the future to one side of his forked identity. Only Ralph himself now resembled a stranger, thanks to that fixed in time vignette of the arm drawn back, confetti bomb poised.

Ralph lingered for a long time with the portrait and its memories before dragging himself away. There was nothing else to do, so he made himself a coffee, taking it with him to Blane's Den, as he was not sure he wanted to be the first thing they all saw on returning home.

Ralph was still in the Den when he heard the family returning. First to seek him out was Kate. Looking him squarely in the face, and taking his hand, Kate said, "Dear Ralph, thank you for coming today. You didn't have to, but I appreciate it. I'm so sorry you've been in the wars. Do you think the healing has started?"

"Well, it was what Blane's hero the Duke would have called a 'Damned close-run thing.' As for healing, I think it's a bit early to say. But look here, Kate, I feel rotten about inflicting myself on you, on the children more especially. Why don't I just vanish, get out of your hair?"

Kate was about to reply when two small faces poked around the door. Jane flicked a glance in Ralph's direction before ducking away. But Jack marched up to Ralph with, "I say! Did you head the goalpost instead of the ball?"

For the first time in over a month, Ralph actually heard himself laugh. It hurt, but it also reassured. "Something like that, Jack. Anyway, it's good to see you kids. Tell me where you're up to with school."

Genevieve alone was formal and withdrawn in Ralph's presence. With his upbringing and latter day lifestyle, he had not gone in much for intuitive thoughts; yet now he sensed in Kate's mother a holding back which had nothing to do with Ralph or Ralph's changed appearance, but suggested there might be some sort of secret she was painfully pushing down.

Came the evening and Edward suggested they should be getting on the road. Kate at once jumped in. "But I'd like Ralph to stay for a day or two. Would that be okay with you, Ralph?"

"Oh but ..."

"No, no, I won't hear any buts. I've still got half a wardrobe of Blane's stuff including at least one new toothbrush, so I promise, you'll want for nothing. And you, Edward, what about you?"

Edward said that he would have to get back home as he had vital appointments the following day. He could always come back south in a day or so to collect Ralph.

The following day, a Sunday, was largely spent at the kitchen table where Kate wanted to quiz Ralph about the accident while coffee was drunk in endless relays. Ralph told Kate about the choice he had been offered, to go for further surgery or discharge with what was left to him. Kate looked Ralph in the face, simply saying, "I think you've made a brave choice. I suppose you can always change your mind in the future."

Into the evening they all watched the television, or rather sat facing the set. Ralph was able to help Jane with a history essay needed for the morning while, at the same time, playing a game of chess with Jack. In the meantime Genevieve bustled in and out of the room without obvious purpose.

Ralph slept badly. Blane's pyjamas were sizes too big, while still managing to scratch him in the area of his groin. It occurred to him that this was the first time he had slept under the same roof as Kate, yet the thought gave him no comfort. The last of his thoughts before drifting off to sleep was, "Will I ever sleep beside a woman again?"

....

The following morning Kate had just returned from taking Jane and Jack to school when a heavy knock sounded on the front door of the house. Answering the knock Kate found she was looking at a robustly built man wearing a peaked hat which he declined to remove. "You would be Mrs Farley?" The man's tone was more of a statement than a question.

"Yes, I'm Kate Farley. Who are you please?"

"I'm from the Bailiff's Office of the County Court and I have a warrant here to remove goods to the value of £391, two and sixpence."

"I don't understand. I think you must have the wrong house."

The bailiff - it transpired his name was Travers - thrust a fold of papers towards Kate while edging towards the open door. "No mistake, Madam, I can assure you. Presuming Mr Blane Farley to be your husband, he has failed to satisfy a County Court judgement at the suit of this finance company - see, it's written down here. As a result my office has been instructed to execute a warrant for possession of goods on these premises. If I may just come in I can let you see what the warrant states." And with that, the man Travers slid his way over the threshold while waving his paperwork in Kate's face.

Her voice rising with a note of hysteria, Kate protested, "I really don't know what this is all about, but I want you to leave my house immediately."

"I'm very sorry, Madam, but I believe you invited me to come in."

"Mrs Farley did no such thing!" From his seat in the kitchen Ralph had heard every exchange between Kate and the bailiff, and he now strode to the door, limbs tensed for action, thankful for once that he was not wearing a mask. "For your information, Mr Farley died two weeks ago and was buried in Deering Churchyard this Saturday gone, so you can take your warrant away with you and stuff it where the sun don't shine. Mrs Farley would like you to leave now. I am a witness to the fact she did not invite you to enter this property."

Staring bemusedly at Ralph, the bailiff retreated over the threshold. He might have been thinking, if this gent is Mr Farley, them gravediggers didn't do too good a job. Instead he said, "All right, all right, keep your wig on! We'll need to report back to the office. If there's been any mistake made, the lady will be informed in due course."

Ralph stepped out after the bailiff and watched while the man got into his car and drove away. "What an extremely unpleasant man!" Ralph took Kate's arm which was shaking violently, and steered her back to a chair in the kitchen.

"Thank God you were here, Ralph. I don't know what I would have done without your help. Trouble is, I know nothing about our financial affairs. For all I know, Blane may have had what do you call it, cash-flow problems. I suppose I should be talking to Edward about it."

"But?"

"But, do I really want to be beholden to my mind controller of a brother?"

Mel and Cerys

A month had passed since Mel had opened her door to find Kate looking down on her with her three inches of superior height, her face a mask of rectitude. That month had found Mel in a strange, a haunted place.

Now Mel forced herself to take a long, a searching look at herself in the mirror. She knew all too well what she did not have. On top of losing the only Playboy, she had now lost Blane, Blane who had made her laugh, Blane who had painted a rainbow. The much harder question was, "What do I have?" Of course there was Keelie, Mel had her mother, not two miles away south of the river. When Keelie was in the country, which was not that often, they exchanged telephone calls though these calls tended to be less conversations, more mother monologues. Vaguely Keelie knew there had been a man in her daughter's life for the last year or more, yet she had never bothered to dig for detail. As a result the name "Blane" was unknown to her, as was Blane's death. For Keelie, career was all.

"Career," Mel thought ruefully. Her own career had hardly set the Thames on fire. Leaving her Comprehensive School with little to show for it, though still inspired by her father's lifelong affair with theatre, she had cast around for a time, looking for introductions to his world. Nothing had turned up. Instead, Mel had drifted into secretarial work with one of the government's ministries. There she had found no challenge other than hopeless attempts to make her boss laugh. When it came down to it, Mel concluded, finally turning her back on the mirror, she was just too frivolous for words.

So, what to do when consumed by the Blues - or the "Mean Reds," as one of Mel's heroines, Holly Golightly, christened the condition? Well, she thought, she would start by tidying the flat which, she admitted, resembled a tip. Doing the job properly, "bottoming," in the words of her grandmother, meant among other acts of ruthlessness, removing the seats from sofa and chairs. In the case of her best chair, Mel was yanking at the fabric ready to dash the dust away when she spotted something small and silvery winking up at her from a bed of fluff. It was a charm. She took it to the window. There was something engraved on the charm. She needed the light to decipher the initials J and J.

The two clues hit Mel at the same moment. The charm could only belong to the bracelet that Kate had been wearing that day; one of the initials was for Jane, the second "J" was for Jack.

....

It was Sunday and Mel was at Blane's home, secretively pushing the envelope through the letterbox. Half of her would have preferred to post the jewellery back to its owner, but she wanted to be absolutely sure the keepsake arrived safely and intact. The thing after all was precious beyond belief.

Mel was scuttling away from the door when it opened. Standing there was Kate. With the sun full on her unmade-up face, her hair any-old-how, she looked somehow less formidable than the last time the women had met.

Kate called out, "Mel! Don't go please. Wait, have you brought what I think you've brought?" She had the envelope in her hand, feeling its contents. "Please come back. Let me thank you properly."

Caught in two minds Mel turned on her heel, staring back at the older woman. "You must have dropped it down the side of the chair at my flat."

"And I've been turning the house upside down looking for it ever since. Come in and have a coffee with me, with us."

The kitchen had a cosy hum to it, the percolator coughing away to itself. Jane and Jack were sat either side of the table, a chess board between them.

"Children this is Mel, and she's very kindly returned that charm we've all been hunting for. Say hello, please." Mumbling his "Hello," the boy glanced in Mel's direction before quickly returning his gaze to the board and picking up a knight with the gesture of someone with checkmate on their mind. His sister on the other hand turned the whole of her body to look at Mel. There was nothing hostile about her expression, yet it was solemn and, Mel thought, unreadable. "I've seen you before," Jane said.

In the act of pouring the coffee Kate looked over to her daughter. "You must have seen Mel with Daddy. She was helping Daddy with his latest, hmm, last book. Isn't that right, Mel?"

Mel nodded silently, taking care not to look in Jane's direction. "Let's take the coffee into the garden, get some of this gorgeous sun, leave these two to their game," this from Kate. It sounded less of a suggestion, more of a decision.

Settled side by side on the south-facing bench, the women sipped coffee in silence. Eventually Kate said, "How are you, Mel?"

Mel thought about the question, trying for an answer with some spirit in it, trying but failing. "I don't know how I am. I feel," she paused for a breath, "well, empty."

Kate fiddled with her bracelet, finally managing to squeeze the charm back on. "Of course, you haven't got the children to distract you. What about your parents, your Mum - I'll happily lend you mine you know." A wan smile flitted across Mel's face, and was gone. "But I know," Kate continued, "It's not really a laughing matter, is it?"

Mel caught herself before sneaking a thumb towards her mouth in the habit of childhood. "You'll tell me I should be joining my local church or signing up for night school, bettering myself in some way or other?"

"You could do worse." Kate drained her coffee, resting the empty cup on the bench. "Mind you, I may just have an idea."

"Oh yes?"

"Yes, well, you'll have to leave that with me. If it comes of anything, I'll let you know, I'll write."

Mel got up to go. "Please say goodbye to Jane and Jack for me." She was at the bottom of the drive when Kate caught up with her, a hand on the girl's arm. "I just want to say, thank you for making Blane happy."

....

Cerys met Mel off her train. Mel had told her over the phone that she would be wearing a red and white checked dress and carrying an Oxford-blue hold-all, so it was not difficult for Cerys to separate Mel from the rest of the emerging crowd of passengers. To hide the shyness of their first meeting, the women traded banalities until they reached the refreshment room and drew breath.

"So, tell me Mel, what have you done about your work?" Set up with coffees, they sat facing each other across a grimy British Rail table.

"Officially I've been signed off by the doctor for a couple of weeks; some mysterious condition no one's likely to know too much about. That hardly weighs on my conscience as I don't owe them anything. Quite the contrary."

"In case it wasn't explained to you, the link with your friend Kate, I mean, there's another person in the chain, someone Kate knows, someone I came across in hospital. I can't tell you who that is as it would breach professional rules; but that doesn't matter. What matters is, you're in need of a change of scenery, while I always welcome a bit of company, especially when doing my thing on the streets."

As she began to relax into their meeting, Mel studied the older woman. Plain of feature, Cerys' face yet had what Mel could only think of as a "beautiful calm." And there was a fine neatness about her, the austere dress complimenting the swept-back hair. This was not someone Mel would find it difficult to live with for the next two weeks. "Tell me about the Street Pastors then?"

"Officially we're attached to Saint Cuthbert's Church, though that's not something we push at folk, religion I mean. What do we do? We rescue teenage girls who exit the nightclubs often without their shoes but more or less drunk, and guide them to the All-night Bus. We talk with the druggeys hanging around the city centre and sometimes do needle exchanges. One time we even retrieved a five-year-old child from the railway embankment and got him back home before midnight."

"Aren't you afraid, afraid of being attacked or molested?"

"Don't worry, we're on friendly terms with all of the emergency services, police, ambulance et cetera, and we have our personal alarms. And we don't go in for breaking up fights. We've all seen what can happen when the police try to break up a fight - the warring factions can suddenly come together and start attacking the authorities. Just one word of advice though - assuming you'll be happy to come out with me one night. If you've brought something suitable in that bag, you'd be as well dressing down."

Mel was allowed a day and a night to settle in before the two of them took to the streets. Skirting the Square their first encounter was with Neil, a Medical Examiner who Cerys knew from hospital. Neil was on the hunt for Gloria who, minutes before had fled the local nick, intent on a fix. In passing Neil told them he suspected Gloria had run out of places on her body in which to inject herself. "Arms and legs are like pincushions! She'll probably be having a go at her groin by now. I wouldn't mind, but we've been rushed off our feet tonight. I've had an old lad with a bad heart caught trying to shop-lift, plus a mentally challenged young man causing a rumpus outside The Feathers! Anyway, best of luck ladies!"

Away from the bright lights of the Square the streets seemed to Mel to pulse with looming threat. Out of nowhere a gaggle of lads swept towards them, forcing the women to sidestep out of their path. "Ho ho ho! Slags in uniform!" came the passing greeting. Mel wasn't sure whether the downpour of rain made things better or worse.

Abruptly Cerys halted at the doorway of a large department store. Mel closed up to her and nearly tripped over a pair of legs stretched across the pavement. "Henry old chap," Cerys' greeting sounded apologetically cheerful. "You really ought to draw those legs of yours in. There's a Blind guy who walks this way; you don't want to cripple each other, do you?"

Henry roused himself on one arm. "Tell me it's not that Miss Hunter then?"

"Come around to haunt you, Henry. Where have you been for the last week?"

"Went up to me mother's, didn't us. Old cow wasn't there, so we walked back here, without socks."

"How are the blisters?"

"They're okay, but the cramps and the squits are something awful. Pardon my French, Miss," this to Mel.

"So meantime you're NFA?" in an aside to Mel she checked that her companion knew what "NFA" stood for.

"Right on, love, NFA, and they tell me I've got a social disease."

"How come?"

"Result of biting some geezer, wasn't it."

"Mind me asking you," Mel bent to look Henry in the eyes. "But what do you do for money?"

"Why Miss, are you itching to give me some?"

"No," Cerys jumped in, "she's not, we're not. My colleague was just interested, that's all."

"Well, I sells them cyclopediacs to the heducated, don't I - when I can get hold of em that is."

Rain continued to sluice the streets. The city had the taste of stirred up dust, and on its breath the sidling aroma of fried onions reminding Mel dimly, incongruously, of love and onion soup. Cranking up to midnight the soundscape boomed and caterwauled. Across the street from the department store a nightclub was busting the air with the Hollies' "Hey Carrie-Ann", while a short distance away a police Panda was carving the night with its Blues and Twos.

"Do you reckon you're normally fit and healthy, Henry?" Cerys pressed on. "What does your doctor say?"

"Perfect, dear, and I don't have no doctor."

"Are you using, using drugs these days?"

"Oh no, no, no. Filthy stuff."

"Have you had a drink today?"

"Drink? I drink water, the water of life. I love water, don't you, Miss?" this again to Mel.

"Have you had contact with the police recently, Henry?"

"Well, apparently I've been shouting at the general public, which I can't believe! Anyway, I was conducted to their station by some truly lovely police persons. I told them someone must have spiked my coffee with some drug, some poison or other. Otherwise there's no way, no way at all I'd want to shout at anyone. And by the way, these police officers of ours are brilliant, just not enough of them, wouldn't you say, Miss?"

"Are you from here, Henry, or where do you come from originally?" Mel wanted to know.

"Me? I come from Bath, Georgian Bath. Beautiful place, Bath, just flaming beautiful."

"So what do you do when you're in Bath?"

"I plays the harmonica. I'm the best harmonica player in the whole of the South West, whole of England if it comes to that."

"Oh, so should we know your name, your professional name?"

"You will do soon, love; I'm the King of the Buskers down there. Any road, if you happen to see those nice police persons will you apologise to them from me. I would hate," Henry exploded in a miner coughing fit, "I would hate for them to think badly of me."

Around twelve-thirty, back in Cerys' spartan flat, the women sat over cocoa and cornflakes to debrief. "Thanks for your company, Mel. Not bad for a first time. As you noticed, I only got twitchy when you started asking Henry about money."

"But when your pay cheque arrives on the dot at the end of every month, it's easy to take money for granted."

Cerys considered for a moment. "It's hardest for the women, life on the streets. Unless they go on the game, it's a case of the rubbish bins and foraging for a piece of stale fruit or the dregs of a cider bottle. Deep down they know that self-respect lies in home-making and rearing kids, but instead they get into a never-ending cycle of dependency and addiction."

"The men too?"

"Ah well, in a strange way the men often are different. Even in their worst moments you'll find a lot of them still cling to the idea of vocation which bolsters a sense of identity. Take our Henry for example. I don't really know how good a harmonica player he is, yet he has convinced himself he's brilliant. I wouldn't mind betting he earns a tidy whack around the Georgian streets of Bath, and all completely tax-free! No, Mel, it's the women I feel for most, it's the women who are the real victims. They can't fight back against society because they've disowned it in the first place, or it's disowned them - take your pick."

Mel was rapt in thought. "So, where does God fit in? You're part of the Church, you should know."

"There's God, and then again, there's the Church. I'm afraid the two don't always go together. It's enough that God has raised us above the other species, that he's given us choice, that he's given us the gift of empathy. If I didn't believe that, I wouldn't be able to do the Street Pastor thing."

They sat in silence for several minutes while all the clocks of the city sounded out the hour. Eventually Cerys asked, "Is it too soon, or can you say it's beginning to work?"

"What's that?"

"Well, your life, your past is none of my business. I just know that when you got off that train, you were one sad lady. Has it helped at all, seeing the way others exist?"

"Maybe. Maybe it has."

"Come on Mel, if I thought you were seriously, clinically depressed, I would make sure that you referred yourself to the right medical people. Some little time back I had a patient whose face had been half burnt away. That guy had every reason to go under. But you, when you catch yourself in the mirror with those eyes and that firmness of jaw, well, you have every reason to grasp at life, to set out on a new journey, to find your rainbow."

Ralph and the Levers of Money

Ralph was again sat in Blane's Den. Kate was perched at the desk, a jumble of envelopes spread in front of her. "Kate, before we start rummaging through that little lot, I've got to ask you the obvious question."

"Which is?"

"Why aren't we involving Edward to help us deal with Blane's debts? From the little I know about these things you're going to need him to organise the probate. I don't even know whether Blane would have left a will. Do you know?"

Kate drew a deep sigh. "Edward's such an organiser. Off and on, he's been trying to organise me ever since we were young, and he never liked Blane. Let him get his feet under the table with this, and the next we know he'll be dictating where the children go to school once they leave Primary." She banged an arm down on the desk, setting off a discordant jangle from her bracelets.

Ralph ran a finger around the underside of his chin before reminding himself it would only make the itching worse. "Dear Kate, you do realise, this is not my thing. I know a lot about trans-European culture and legal systems in the eighteenth and nineteenth centuries, and I'm not too bad a lecturer and tutor, but the Law and the world of money just ain't my bag. However," touching Kate lightly on the wrist, "I may just have had an idea as to how we can stave off Blane's creditors."

....

North again, Ralph gathered his correspondence with the insurance company, rereading carefully before consigning it to a smart new folder. That correspondence, he realised, was worth money, hard cash. The only problem was, Kate needed money now, whereas his claim for compensation - Edward had termed it damages - could take weeks or even months.

Ralph decided to go headfirst for the bank, the bank with whom he had been a customer for twenty years. The manager was a Mr Jenkinson. Mr Jenkinson was affable enough yet with the air of someone counting the days till retirement and the inflation-proofed bulwark of the bank's generous pension. Ralph, the urgency of the situation uppermost in his mind, was tempted to ask straight out, "Can I borrow money on this?" As it was, and after the usual salutations, he provided a bit of background to his visit before handing his file of correspondence across the desk, inviting the manager to read.

Jenkinson read, punctuating his reading with repeated "Dear me"s. After ten minutes he slowly replaced the paperwork, looked up at Ralph, cleared his throat loudly and asked, "So Mr Ransom, please don't think me rude, and clearly you've had a most distressing experience, but how exactly is this anything to do with the bank?"

"Okay so, I'm clearly going to end up with a hansom pay-out. I'm here to ask whether the bank would be prepared to lend against that pay-out - do you call it a bridging loan?"

Jenkinson removed his spectacles and started polishing vigorously. Eventually, spacing his words with deliberation, he said, "This is not really the sort of business the bank goes in for. Hmm, you will have noted that the company has not admitted liability. The words 'Without Prejudice' appearing at the end of their correspondence, I think you will find, have a certain legal significance." He paused. "So, hmm, Mr Ransom, I'm afraid there's nothing this bank can do for you on this occasion. I sense you may have something, hmm, altruistic in mind." Unscrewing his fountain pen and taking up a notepad he concluded, "So this is the address and phone number of a firm of solicitors here in town. Come what may, you are going to need some legal advice. Tell them the introduction came from me, will you."

The following morning after Edward had left for his office, Ralph telephoned Purchase & co. Solicitors. He gave the girl receptionist his name and asked if he could have an appointment to see Mr Purchase. He was asked, "Are you an existing client of ours, Mr Ransom?" On receiving the reply "No," the girl explained, "Mr Purchase is really quite busy just now. I'm afraid you'd be looking at the week after next at the earliest."

Doing his best to keep his impatience in check, Ralph cut in with, "I've had a serious road smash. The third party's insurers have written to me to settle my claim for compensation which I believe will come to five figures." After muffling the phone for a moment, the girl then came back with, "Sir, it looks as if you may be in luck after all. Mr Purchase has just had an appointment cancelled. Can you come in to us now? Mr Purchase is an expert in your sort of case."

Bouncy, sharp of features, Mr Purchase certainly looked as if he was expert in something. Coming out to meet Ralph in reception, he pumped his visitor's hand energetically before ushering him into his private office. Turning down the offer of coffee, Ralph produced his file, sliding it across the out-sized desk. "I've come about this. I hope you can help me." Up to this point the solicitor had not looked at Ralph. "Well, let us see. All right if I have a bit of a look-see?" The reading of the file proved surprisingly brief. In between pages Mr Purchase sneaked furtive glances at his visitor. His reading done he looked Ralph full in the face for the first time, quickly looking away again. "Sadly Mr hmm Ransom, I fear you have been misinformed. Experts we are, but experts in shipping law, not road traffic. Why don't you try Quilty and Sutherland in the Square?"

Ralph retreated, baffled and angry. He was tempted to just give the thing up, explain to Kate that he had drawn a total blank. Then, brooding over a mug of Edward's most exclusive tea, he had an idea. He would get in touch with Don, the works manager at the County Blind Headquarters and ask whether the Society retained a particular firm of lawyers, tame or otherwise. After all, he, Ralph, had given of his volunteer service for a good four weeks, and that had to be worth at least an introduction.

The idea worked. It turned out that Clive Burrows had not only handled the Society's legal work over a ten-year period; he also happened to be a trustee, something that brought him into contact with the workshop and its denizens on a regular basis.

Ralph met Clive Burrows in the Society's boardroom, the much-trailed file under his arm. At once, he realised with a small thrill, he could have struck lucky for a change. While gripping his hand, the solicitor looked Ralph full in the face without turning away. Clive indicated a chair and then sat down alongside Ralph, there being no desk to come between them. He listened patiently while Ralph related the history of his injuries as well as his idea to come to Kate's rescue having roughly totalled Blane's debts to be in excess of £3,000.

Clive asked questions, asked a lot of questions. After half an hour he stretched back in his chair, faced Ralph and said, "If you're happy with this, Mr Ransom, I can deal with both things, the insurance claim and the probate procedures, and I'll be happy to do this without expecting any sort of a payment on account. Of course, both things will take time, so what I suggest is I write, on my firm's notepaper of course, to each of the creditors to inform them as to what is happening and to provide Solicitor Undertakings where I feel these are needed. That action should kill two birds with the single stone. What I mean is, first off, creditors like nothing worse than being ignored; and number two, a Solicitor's Undertaking goes a heck of a long way, almost as good as cash in the hand. How does that sound to you as a plan?"

Ralph was still thinking what a neat plan had been put to him when a telephone call to Kate to report his progress resulted in a check to his spirit. Kate listened to Ralph's account without interruption. When he was finished, she said meekly, "Oh Ralph, that's wonderful, you're wonderful. Only one problem. How am I ever going to pay you back?"

Melanie

"As from today," Melanie reminded herself, "I am no longer Mel; I am Melanie." This was something that had been prompted, virtually decided for her by Cerys over their final midnight cocoa. Giving out with her natural lemony scent, so delicate it was hard to think of it as artificial, Cerys had lightly touched Mel's wrist with, "If you would be happy with this, I think you should be Melanie from now on. It's a much nicer name than Mel. It's a beautiful name, and it would suit you."

"Where's this coming from?" Mel wanted to know.

Cerys fingered the miniature cross at her neck and thought for a moment. "Kate told me this much; she told me you'd had a friendship with someone who had then died. She didn't say who that someone was or give me any details, and of course I didn't ask. But this was a huge event in your life, a trauma, something that must have turned you upside down and inside out. You have experienced loss and sacrifice, but sacrifice can lead to new birth."

Now Melanie was on the train speeding back south. The train was busy with fractious children and flustered mothers, though none disturbed Melanie, coiled as she was in a corner with her thoughts.

At Leicester she briefly glanced out of the window. Standing tall from the platform a bill board proclaimed, "Filbert Street - Home Of The Foxes." At the bottom in jazzy script ran the legend, "Back Of The NET!!" In between, a leaping "Freddie Fox" kitted out in football boots and royal blue shirt. "Back-of-the-net," she thought, "If life was only that simple." The train jerked forward again.

There was something else Cerys had said. She searched her mind. Yes, she'd said, "Each of us has at least one precious thing that can't be bought with money nor nurtured by wealth or the trappings of station or status, things that are no more than skin-deep. Even Henry, remember, has his prowess with the harmonica. But it's devotion that's the key. Devotion's the key that will keep that one precious thing alive, alive and growing." Melanie knew deep down this was true because her Dad had brought her up with the fable of the orphan boy and his blood red rose. She had lost one precious thing, the gift of bringing happiness to one precious person; yet the baton had been handed back to her by Blane himself and his, "Always look for the rainbow and the gold at rainbow's end."

Rainbows of course did not come around to order. She had the sense to know that. There would be a period - it might be a long period - of treading water, feeling her way. She could not duck it, she was lonely, and Cerys' promise that, "One day love will banish loneliness" barely cut it. "But hey!" she remembered, "I'm Melanie now!" She snoozed as far as Luton.

....

Melanie was back at her desk in the Department's typing pool of junior officers. Nothing there had changed over the period of her unofficial leave, since her stay with Cerys, not that she expected anything different. One floor down her group leader still refused to engage with her sense of humour, while the girls either side of her in the pool continued trying to persuade her it was her turn to make the tea.

Humour? It was not that Melanie felt there was that much of a cue for humour just now. Her time in the north with Cerys had been important. It was the first time she had felt remotely close to another human being since Blane, for that was what Cerys was, a most human being. Harder though it was to accept, she also felt obscurely grateful to Kate for making the introduction. Yet Melanie could not tell herself she was content. The spirit, the spirit of that Playgirl who had fired her teenage years to return thanks to Blane, that spirit seemed to have left her in body and in soul. What remained, the tedious workaday routines of life, stretched out before her in the flattest of flat lines.

On her second day back, Melanie's working life started as it started most mornings, with her plucking a mini cassette from the stand on her desk and slapping it into her tape deck. Fully expecting it to be the latest dictation from one of the grey men on the floor below, she adjusted her earphones and pulled her Olivetti towards her. The tape was playing when her intercom buzzed and she was bidden downstairs to collect some paperwork urgently needed on the floor above. Before cutting off the tape Melanie just had time to register that it was not meant for transcription, by her, possibly by anyone.

Returning to her desk ten minutes later she was about to eject the tape and choose another when something she had heard at the same time as the intercom buzzer tickled back to her early morning brain. "Playboy," she had definitely heard the word "Playboy." Alerted by the familiar phrase and curious despite herself, she spun the tape back and listened from the beginning.

Through her earphones Melanie heard a pleasant but unfamiliar female voice intone, "Hello there! This is to let you know that you are someone my boss has admired from afar for some time. My boss would very much like to meet you away from the office and for the next two lunchtimes will be found in the books department of Hamley's on Regent Street choosing something for a young nephew, *Playboy Magazine* under the arm for easy recognition. My boss very much hopes you will keep the *rendez-vous*."

Melanie sat staring at her dictaphone while the tape wound on silently. Was this some sort of joke? It wasn't her birthday; it wasn't even April 1st. Was the message, the assignation intended for her in the first place? The pleasant-sounding voice had offered no name, and there were hundreds of people in the building. No, Melanie decided, it had to be a spoof, either that or a reckless case of mistaken identity. She tossed the tape aside and plucked a replacement after checking she had remembered to bring a sandwich for her midday break. But for the rest of the day and overnight the stupid thing refused to exit her brain, and in the morning she left for work without packing her lunch.

Melanie had never in her life been to the world-famous toy store, although she knew exactly where it was. Hamley's was as close as could be to the equally famous Jaeger shop whose windows she had longingly peered through a time or two. Curiosity had finally got the better of her. After all, what had she got to lose? And it was not as if she was invited to the arches of Charing Cross at midnight. What could possibly be more wholesome, more innocent than the book department of Hamley's at lunchtime?

As Melanie turned to enter the store she was greeted on either side by a jovial phalanx of clowns, each nodding and ho-hoing in her general direction, face masks vaguely sinister in their dead white paint. Through the doors the place vibrated with life. To one side a radio-controlled aeroplane - it could have been a Spitfire - was being demonstrated to the delight of a gaggle of ten-year-olds; opposite a giant teddy bear was talking squeakily to a toddler with a rapt and entranced expression on her face; In between an elaborate model railway layout occupied centre stage. To a child, she decided, the soundscape must be a melody of joy and anticipation.

Melanie tracked down the book department to the first floor rear. The centre of the room was dominated by a display of the latest *Biggles* featuring the long-running adventures of W.E. Johns' flying policeman. Having no idea whether she was early or late to confront her mystery admirer, be they admirer or prankster, she took to drifting round the shelves, studying the titles with just part of her attention. A minute or two of this and Melanie out of the corner of her eye spotted a red and gold head scarf edging around the *Biggles* display and, yes, a magazine sticking out from an arm. She turned around quickly to look for the *Playboy* logo.

As far as her imagination had been able to take her, Melanie had expected to be confronted by a man, probably middle-aged, probably grey-haired, someone who, a little like Blane, was in need of bringing fantasy to life. In the event, her "admirer" turned out to be a woman, a shortish compact woman with a slightly pixyish quizzical face and startling violet eyes.

"Melanie! I was sure you would come. I'm Veronica, Ronnie to my friends. Now, how about some proper lunch for once. You must be tired of that daily sandwich of yours. They know me at The Ivy and the Savoy Grill, so which might you prefer?"

They were moving, Ronnie tucking Melanie's arm in hers. Only one of the clowns remained on duty at the doors of the store. Was Melanie imagining it or did the white face wink? Out again on the bustling pavement Ronnie flagged down a black cab and together they bundled into the back.

A short ride and they were outside the Savoy Grill. Melanie had time only to take in the dazzling white of the table cloths along with the fine perfume of wine in the air. They were greeted effusively by George, the maître d'hôtel and shown to a corner table by an immaculate waiter who also recognised Ronnie. Scooping up the menu with a flourish Ronnie said, "Ah! That's good, they've got the Lemon Sole on today. I do recommend the Lemon Sole with, perhaps a glass or two of their Riesling."

Melanie at last managed to catch her breath. "This is all very exciting, do you know, but do you mind me asking, who are you?"

The same waiter was hovering at Ronnie's elbow. She gave the waiter their order. "Damn fair question, Melanie. So, I am a Second Permanent Secretary back at the factory, though not in your department. You're wondering, 'Woman - Second Permanent Secretary?' Well true, there aren't many of us to the pound. Many more in the future I'm thinking."

For the first time Melanie looked up and into the other woman's face. A suggestion of wrinkles around those magnificent eyes told she was older than Melanie had thought to begin with. Yet seen as a piece the pixy face shone out with naked intelligence and youthful energy. "So does that mean you can make excuses for me when I roll back late for the afternoon shift?"

Ronnie reached over and lightly touched Melanie on the wrist. "Already sorted, my dear. You've been out delivering important documents across town, and you got held up in this hellish traffic of ours."

The wine arrived and they clinked glasses. "Here's to my idea," Ronnie was looking across the table with a disconcertingly frank gaze. "I've been watching you for a month or two, and to cut to the chase, I want to recruit you as my personal assistant. There are just too many men in our place and I'd welcome a bit of feminine company."

Melanie stayed silent, playing with her napkin. Then she said, "But if you don't mind me asking, why the cloak and dagger stuff? Could you not have gone through - what do you call it - the usual channels?"

They sat back as their meal was served. "Clever girl, yes of course I could have done things by the book, but I hate having to bow and scrape to those awful men in Treasury, so I'm doing it my way for once. Besides which, I admit it, I was curious to see how you would react to my little subterfuge." Ronnie paused to savour the first mouthful of her fish. "Now, I'll tell you what I'll do, because I know you will want a little time to think things over, yes? I'll record a cassette of how I see your job working, what it will call for from you, what we would reckon to pay, and all that boring stuff. You can think it over and then perhaps we can meet again for another lunch. How does that sound to you, Melanie? But please, don't say anything now; let's just enjoy this sole - up to their usual high standard if I'm not mistaken."

Finished off with coffees, the meal all too soon was ending. The women were getting up to leave the Grill when Ronnie asked, "Oh, and by the way my dear, have you ever been on the stage?"

Ralph and the Face of the Future

Ralph had had quite enough of living with Edward. Edward had provided sanctuary at a bad time in Ralph's life, and Ralph was grateful for that; but now he was stronger, at least he thought he was stronger, and could do without the endless quizzing:- "Have you decided yet where you're going with your damages claim?" and "Are you reconsidering the offer of further surgery?" and "You do know, don't you, Blane Farley, your Etonian chum, was really a bit of a rat, quite a lot of a rat come to that, feet of clay, you know?"

So it was that after six months or so, Ralph purchased a modest set of wheels, and moved back to his flat at the university. Back to teaching? Ralph didn't know. That would have to wait. He would choose his moment before bearding the Vice Chancellor in his ivory tower.

On the credit side of life's balance sheet, Ralph was two important notches to the good. He was doing things for himself once again, and he was no longer turning his mirror to the wall. "Mirror image" was no longer something to be avoided. He was finding he could even make faces at himself. The only trouble was that word "Self." He remembered a line from a poem that went something like, "The self that I knew is in focus no longer." Was his still the face of the man who had conquered the playing fields of his youth and charmed a generation of undergraduates from Carfax to the Woodstock Road? or was it the face of a stranger?

Ralph thought of those masters of espionage, the spies who enlivened his lighter reading, characters such as George Smiley. For as long as thirty years or more, such characters found it necessary to reinvent themselves, to clothe themselves around new identities, bolstered by new narratives to new lives. How on earth did they manage to relate to the people, the landmarks of a once familiar world? The only answer Ralph could come up with was the eyes, the one feature, the one focus above all to which people looked for truth and individuality. Yes, he decided, from now on it was his eyes that would have to launch his new self.

....

One morning Ralph was sat staring at the deplorable state of his flat when a ring came at his front door. He ignored it. The ring came again. With a sigh he stirred himself and padded over to the hall in his bare feet. He was not used to visitors.

Stood in the doorway was Kate. "Ralph my dear, remember, I threatened you with a visit, but let me in quickly, I'm dying for the loo!"

Retreating, Ralph pointed the way to his bathroom before feverishly attacking islands of mess in the living room. "Gosh! That's better!" Kate emerged from the bathroom, smoothing down her shirt. "Thank you dear boy, now let me explain. I'm on my way north to spend a couple of days with my Godmother. She's one lovely lady, but she's not getting any younger, and it's ages since I saw her last. Anna's got the kids, so I'm a free agent for once."

"It's great to see you, Kate. Sorry about the tip," this with a despairing gesture towards the room at large. "Here, I'll just shift these mags and you'll have somewhere to sit down. When did you eat last? Can I take you out for a late lunch?"

"Thanks, but I'm fine, stoked up with a good breakfast before setting off. Besides which, I wanted to see you, to see how you are - never so easy if you're juggling menus."

"So, how do I look?" Ralph put a heavy emphasis on the "do."

Looking straight into Ralph's face, Kate took her time. "Not bad, not too bad at all," she paused. "If a little on the pale side. Tell you what, why don't you take me for a quick tour of your campus, after which you can give me a coffee, and I'll be on my way."

The day sparkled after the heavy dew of the morning. They strode out together, Ralph pointing out the more important landmarks as they went. Rounding a tall stand of oaks, they came in view of the great tower which had been gifted to the university along with much of the grounds by its illustrious patron. Spears of sunlight glanced off the windows of the tower, and danced across the lake beneath. Not for the first time, Ralph detected a significance, a symbolism about the dominating structure which was far greater than the sum of its bricks and mortar.

Back at his flat, Ralph headed for the kitchen and the coffee pot. "Hang on, that will wait," Kate was in charge. "Come with me to the bathroom." In the bathroom Kate sat Ralph down on a stool in front of the mirror. "Will you let me do something about that pallor?" Without waiting for a reply she delved into her bag to disgorge a tumble of powders and paints. "Now, be a good boy and stay as still as you can." With frequent glances back to the mirror, Kate then proceeded to transform Ralph's face, giving colour to the flaccid cheeks and powdering around the skin grafts where they joined. Ralph submitted. Once he all but laughed, remembering back to childhood and his mother's attempts to clean him up after some chocolate centred indulgence. As it was, he gave himself up to the sensation of the moment, the firmness of her fingers beneath his chin, the sweetness of her breath an inch away.

....

The meeting with the Vice Chancellor and Ralph's head of department took place. Unashamedly Ralph prepared with his own brand of making up. It was not as good as Kate's creation but, he thought, it passed.

The detail of the meeting went by in a blur and was remembered afterwards by Ralph for the soothing soundtrack of Vaughan Williams' Pastoral Symphony flooding softly from an open window. The details, he was assured, could be confirmed later by letter. Meantime, he understood, the faculty would be happy to retain his services provided he felt up to it. There was no issue with the courses Ralph had been teaching for the last few years; yet the suggestion was put to him that he might consider striking out with a fresh subject. To give him the necessary time to prepare, a further suggestion was made that he could take a term's leave of absence in order to work up materials. Ralph immediately grasped at both propositions. Already he had started to sketch out ideas for a First Year course on the origins and legacies of the French Revolution.

Now he was on the ozone-high passenger deck of the P. & O. ferry, looking back towards those iconic White Cliffs and forward to the smudge of Cap Gris Nez, new colour, fresh tang of salt waters flooding his senses.

Some minutes into the crossing Ralph felt an arm slip through his. Kate had been down to the Duty-Free, returning festooned with packages. "This is a lovely sight, a lovely feeling. Don't you still get a thrill when you're starting out on a journey?" this to a chorus of excited seagulls, and a booming reverberation of the ship's siren.

Ralph licked the salt from his lips, and turned into his companion. "I suppose I do. Mind you, the thrill will be just as great if they ever get round to building a tunnel. Anyway, you were going to tell me where you learned your French?"

"Okay, so you've heard me talk about my friend Anna? Well Anna and her husband Paul have an au pair, Maddie, who came to them some years ago and then took root. Maddie's bilingual and gives French language lessons on a more or less informal basis. It was one of the things I decided to challenge myself with after Blane. Six months on, Maddie says I'm pretty good, though just how far I'll be able to help you with your research remains to be seen!"

"Oh don't worry. It's jolly sporting of you to do this at all. I'm most grateful."

"Rubbish, Mr Ransom, you helped me out by staving off Blane's creditors and keeping the bailiffs away. This is very little in return." Kate paused. "So long as you don't mind the older woman as an escort!"

....

On their first full day in the French capital, Ralph and Kate descended on the Sorbonne, Paris' venerable university. Ralph was armed with a letter of introduction from his department which he hoped would open doors, and of course archives. To an extent this worked, though the assistance they received was grudging at best. Kate did what she could with the materials they were able to access; though as she admitted, the language was stretching her. Ralph had explained that it would be easy enough to construct his new course relying simply on secondary sources; yet in his world it was a bit like cheating or selling his students short were he to fail to quote original texts and up to date analysis.

Sensing they were making very slow progress, Ralph suggested they adjourn for lunch, and they chose a pavement cafe around the corner from the Opera. Although the service was a little on the surly side, the food, which included an exquisite tomato salad, was appetising, while the sunshine went some way towards restoring their spirits. Relaxing over coffee and cognac, they were content to watch the world go by in drifts of Cap Bleu, reminding Ralph of holidays in his student days. No wonder, Kate mused, that "*flâneur*" was a French expression, a Gallic concept.

They were getting up to leave after dealing with *L'addition* when a trio of neighbourhood boys rolled and swaggered by their table. One of the lads looked back at Ralph and in a loud voice announced to the world, "Hey! *Regardez donc ce bouffon!*" Ralph asked Kate for a translation, but was told she had not quite caught the gist.

Instead of going back to the Sorbonne they took to strolling the boulevards, Ralph promising himself he would look through his notes later. Before they knew it, the afternoon had gone, dissolved in sunshine and mild alcoholic haze. Sad that the day was coming to an end, they slowed their steps back to the Trocadero and their lodging.

Happier than he had felt for a long time, Ralph showered before collapsing into bed, wondering whether his second night's sleep would turn out to be as calm and dreamless as the first. An hour or so into it he knew the answer as he found he was sitting bolt upright in the bed, scrabbling for light and sweating like a trooper on the march. It was that nightmare again, the nightmare of being trapped in the flaming torch of a leaky four-by-four, fighting to get out, fighting to stay alive.

The bedroom door opened. Dimly Ralph was aware of Kate silhouetted in the doorway, Kate coming up to stand beside the bed. "Hey Ralph, it's okay, it's okay. I could hear you from next door. You were shouting out, something about a bridge. You were obviously having a nightmare. Was it about your accident? Hang on, I'll give us a bit of light."

Ralph shuffled his body under the bed clothes. "Not too much, please, and I'm sorry that I woke you."

Kate fumbled her way to the bedside lamp which shed a subdued orange light. After closing the bedroom door she lay down on top of the bed. She felt for Ralph's hand, but could not find it, so instead she reached out for his face, kissing him briefly on his lips and, ever so gently stroking his cheek.

Ralph had no idea how long they lay like this, the sweetness of her breath going in time with his own. Eventually he said, "*Bouffon* means clown, doesn't it?"

"Yes my dear, it does, but that doesn't mean you're a clown. Clowns hide behind their masks; you might have wanted to hide for a time, but that's over now, now you're coming out into the light."

"Are you saying I'm not as ugly as Joseph Merrick, 'Elephant Man'?"

"Hah! I seem to have heard somewhere, though he smelled a bit, he was a wow with the ladies."

"So you don't think I should follow in the steps of that pop group, take up my begging bowl and find a new home on the banks of the Ganges?"

"Live the holistic life, you mean? I know we're told that Eastern ways of treating mind and body are superior to Western chemical solutions, but I don't think you're quite ready to embrace Buddhism and the Middle Way."

Ralph eased a hip sideways, releasing an arm to curve around Kate's shoulder. "Don't know about that. Though come to think of it, doesn't their faith teach suppression of the ego, restraint of the senses and the way of the world? - 'Right view; Right aim; Right speech; Right actions; Right living; Right effort; Right mindfulness; Right concentration,' hoping I've remembered the important bits. Mind you, Kate, if you think I once had an ego as big as a house, you're not wrong; but I reckon I left it behind in that fireball along with ego's ugly twin? ..."

"Which is?"

"The everyday familiarity that breeds self-delusion. Finding your ultimate purpose in life is not easy if you have to rely on the Siren world of the ego. As a wise man once said, you are never the same person after you've looked over the edge of the Grand Canyon ..."

"Which is just what I've been trying to tell you. You've looked over the edge and you've survived. What's that phrase? ..."

"Yes I know, 'What doesn't kill, makes men stronger'."

A sudden burst of rain rattled the windows of the bedroom.

Edward Confesses

Ralph woke one morning to find that he had again overslept. The problem was his alarm clock which had mysteriously gone missing. Then it had come to him; he could only have left it behind when moving out from Edward's house. The thought made Ralph smile. On leaving Edward he had fully expected to have an inventory thrust at him with a "Sign here!" demand. As it was, Edward had of course been punctilious about reclaiming the house key lent to Ralph with due ceremony months before.

A phone call to Edward followed by a return call proved Ralph's theory correct. It seemed the clock had got tucked under the bed allocated to him for the duration of his stay *chez* Upchurch. Ralph was about to ask if Edward could post the item to him when Edward broke in with, "As it happens, old chap, I'm due to see a client in your neck of the woods, so I don't mind dropping it in for you. Can't have you getting up late for your lectures, can we?"

Edward arrived at Ralph's door early one September morning, redolent of leaf mould and wood smoke. Ralph was only half dressed, so that, despite himself, he found he was apologising to his guest. Waiving the apology aside, Edward strode to the centre of the living room. Clamping a hand on each hip, he raised his small head and sniffed, a blood hound scenting a quarry. "I smell perfume."

Ralph hesitated, reluctant to share his private affairs. In the end he said, "That can only be down to your sister Kate. She flew in here for a pit stop a while back, en route for her Godmother up north. That perfume of hers is distinctive, but I'd no idea it was still hanging around. You know what my sinuses are like."

"Oh, right, so you like to keep in touch with Big Sis, do you? Me thinks perhaps there may be things concerning our family that you need to know about."

Realising he was not going to get rid of Edward straight away, Ralph suggested, "Okay then, how about a bracing walk? around the campus? I've nothing on until a tutorial after lunch."

The men set out on what was to prove the first of several laps of the circuit. Still savouring a recent, more intimate walkabout, Ralph was not really in the mood to act tourist guide; yet he need not have worried on that account as Edward showed scant interest, and was even unimpressed by the great tower looming up four-square through the morning mist.

"You must know by now, Kate and I, well, we've always been close. I suppose it goes right back to schooldays when, as I thought of it, we were deliberately split up. Kate stayed at home and went to the local day school while I was shipped off to Merelles, Merelles Academy."

Ralph moodily kicked out at a stone in the path, wondering with half his mind what might be coming next. "Yes okay, I know Merelles."

"Don't mind telling you, Ralph, I fairly hated the place, the cold baths, the stink of the boot room, all the things you probably revelled in being the Hearty that you are. And the boys, the boys were simply hateful, sons of farmers and nouveau-riche factory owners, most of them. Don't mind telling you, they played some pretty mean tricks. Because I was smaller than them they saw an easy target. Many a time I would find myself surrounded by a jeering, baiting ring, chanting things like, 'Upchurch's so wet, you wouldn't find him if he fell in the river! Shall we throw you in the river, Upchurch, see if you float?'"

Just then they rounded a bend in the path, nearly colliding with a group of undergraduates. One of the students, a fresh-faced girl, turned around, smiled broadly at Ralph, and assured him her essay on Robespierre would be in his pigeonhole by the weekend.

Back in step, Edward continued. "So, where were we? Ah yes, fast forward to the day that Kate came to the school with the parents. I'd been writing home for some time, saying how much I was missing her. Can't remember now whether it was a Red Letter day, other than for me; doesn't matter. What mattered was, Kate fell into the clutches of Henshaw Major, known to us boys as 'Hitler,' due to his looking a bit like Adolf, minus the moustache of course. From our first term at Merelles Henshaw had been one of my baiters-in-chief, and now he saw his chance to tighten the screw. Offering to show Kate the school, Henshaw managed to get her away from the parents. What happened then - something or nothing - well, I never really knew. I just knew that Kate reappeared later, looking extremely upset, red in the cheek, hair all over the place."

"Yep, I can see how you must have felt. But ..."

"Hang on, Ralph, I'm getting to the end of this bit of the story. After the Henshaw episode it came to me one morning in chapel. I had to do something, achieve something that would make Kate proud of me, make it so that she would not want to leave my side the next time she visited. Trouble was, there was nothing at all sexy that I was good at. Getting nineteen out of twenty for a history essay wasn't likely to cut it."

"What did you come up with?"

"So, it was three weeks away from the annual blue ribond event, the steeplechase over a course that took the runners right around the grounds, something over a mile in length. Each day after lessons I started training, not minding how many people saw me at it. In the process I got to know literally every twist and turn of the course. In a word, I found a spot where I might hope to take a short-cut without being caught in the act. Came the big day, and my plan worked out to perfection. I romped home, breasting the tape ahead of all those fancied runners! Kate of course was there, and she was the first to rush up to hug and congratulate me!" Edward paused for emphasis. "But ..."

"Yes, I thought there was going to be a but."

"Another boy, name of Bloomfield - he'd been dogging my heels from the Starter's gun - he followed in my tracks at the point I dived off on my short cut. Bloomfield knew I had cheated. As far as I know he said nothing to anyone until, years later and many thousands of miles away, he spilled the beans, to Blane Farley of all people!"

Breaking stride, Ralph pulled up and stared at Edward. "How the hell did that happen?"

"Well of course, you know all about the Gloucesters. Weren't you keen on following Blane into the regiment at one time? You'll know all about the 'Glorious Gloucesters' and their heroic doings in Korea. I'm told they are the only outfit to sport two cap badges, one at the front, one at the back, marking the time they were virtually surrounded by the enemy and had to fight like the devil to survive."

"I know the story."

"So, as Blane took pleasure in telling me years later, he was dug in at an outpost atop a hill with just an under-strength platoon including a single subaltern. That subaltern happened to be Bloomfield. As the two of them stood-to in the dark watches of the night, waiting for the Chinese and chucking dead rats into no-mans-land, they got to swapping tales about their schooldays. Don't ask me exactly how it came out; but one tale obviously led to another, and the truth about that steeplechase fell into Blane's hands like a pearl."

The two men stepped out again. "So, how did you get to know about this?" Ralph's interest was at last kindled.

"Okay, so, now we come to the really nasty part of the whole thing. The cowardly secret laid buried for years. Then one day - I'll never forget it because the temperature was up in the nineties - Blane called on me at my office. He was having more money problems and he thought I could help. You see, he was counting on my, well my closeness to Kate. Scoundrel thought I would never wish Kate and the children any sniff of poverty. Anyway, you'd agree, Ralph, wouldn't you, normally Blane would be the last person to discard jacket and tie, but this day was different because of the heat. When he left the office to take a leak his jacket remained behind on the back of his chair."

"So no doubt you couldn't resist a little look-see?"

"Fraid so, old chap. And what did I find tucked to the back of his wallet? Only a snap of a young girl, and quite a looker at that! Scrawled on the back of the photograph were a few words of code. Can't tell you what they said, but they were clearly some sort of endearment."

"Did you challenge Blane there and then?"

Edward broke away momentarily to allow a pair of runners to jog by. Looking away from Ralph and down the hill in the direction of the tower, he replied, "No, I didn't, though I wish now that I had. I don't know, I suppose I wanted to weigh up the implications. In which direction lay the greater hurt for Kate?"

"But something tells me I'm not going to hear a happy ending to this story."

"The sleeping dogs kept sleeping for a year or so. Then one day - I remember I'd just got back to my office following a lengthy audit of a local firm's iffy accounts - out of the blue Blane was on the phone. Of course it was about money again. I'm afraid I lost it somewhat, told him exactly what I thought of him. Blane hit back, accusing me of being a cheat and regaling me with Bloomfield's revelations on that Korean hill top, not something Kate would be too impressed by, he warned. And, you've guessed it, I just had to retaliate, charging him with having an affair with a girl half his age, a girl I now can put a name to, by the way! That was the end of our, hmm, conversation. I thought he had put the phone down on me. I found out later he was dying."

Melanie in Denmark

Ronnie dropped a hand on to Melanie's arm and fixed her with her most winning smile. They were in Ronnie's office, and Melanie was handing over a pile of photo stats before leaving work for the day and returning to her less than welcoming flat. "My dear, is your passport up to date?" Melanie replied that it was.

While busily rummaging through the papers on her desk, Ronnie explained. "It seems that our lords and masters wish us to talk with our friends in Copenhagen. It's all to do with bacon and butter and quotas. Naturally I'll need to have my trusted Girl Friday by my side so, you up for it? We'll be travelling First Class of course. We can fly naturally, but for once I thought we might take a few days of leave and go overland. Apart from anything else, we've been so busy, I've hardly had a chance to get to know my Playgirl!"

They sailed overnight from Harwich on the British Rail ferry *Avalon*, breakfasting well on bacon and eggs before boarding their train at Hook van Holland. Sharing a cabin with another woman was a new experience for Melanie; yet Ronnie had been at pains to avoid possible embarrassments while proving she was no snorer. Unusually for October, the North Sea had obliged with a calm crossing.

Rotterdam was soon behind them, Bremen and Hamburg ahead. They had their First Class compartment to themselves, so Ronnie felt free to gossip merrily about the Department and her ongoing battles with colleagues, almost exclusively male. As the tulip fields flashed passed the windows, she quipped, "What's said on the Boat Train stays on the Boat Train - yes?"

As the express powered eastwards across the North German Plain, Melanie ventured a word in edgeways and a change of subject. "When you took me for that wonderful meal at the Savoy, you asked me whether I'd ever appeared on stage. Do you mind me asking, what was that about?" This with a hint of the Irish in the question.

Ronnie reached across from her window seat, touching Melanie lightly on the arm. "Of course I don't mind. We're on holiday; ask anything you want. It just so happens I'm a patron of the Royal Court out Hammersmith way. The theatre's always on the look out for new young talent. I thought with your classical Celtic looks and that dancing voice, you might have been tempted, you might be tempted to - what's the modern expression? - strut your stuff - no?"

Melanie's mouth fell open momentarily. She had no instant reply. Ronnie's question had taken her back more than ten years, taken her back to those magical evenings when father and daughter had fired back and forth at each other in the guise of Christie Mahon and Pegeen Mike, while waiting for wife and mother to return home. But that had been such a private thing, strictly a Two-hander, as her Dad termed it. Outside the home there had been nothing of that sort, not a single opportunity.

"You know, I could easily sign you up for a workshop or two. Would you like that?"

In her head, Melanie was still in County Sligo, County Sligo morphing into the Austrian Tyrol. Embarrassed, she had to ask Ronnie to repeat her question.

"I just thought it would be nice for you to try it out, and meet some interesting new people at the same time. I'd be happy to take you along and introduce you. Anyway, think about it, why don't you?"

They each dozed for a time. Then they were pulling into the station at Lubeck. "An hour and a bit on the ferry, and we'll be on Danish soil," Ronnie explained. "By the way, I've yet to tell you, but we're not booked into any hotel. We're the invited guests of old friends of mine in Copenhagen. Ola and Mariett are a charming couple, and they'll be meeting us off the ferry."

"Hey look!" Melanie looked up to see a skein of Brent Geese over-flying the ferry in perfect arrow formation, the drumming of their wings filling the autumn sky.

....

Ola and Mariett lived in a rambling turn-of-the-century house on the outskirts of the Danish capital. They had a family of sons aged either side of twenty who, it seemed, came and went with a casualness to which their parents were well adjusted. Apart from Ola and Mariett themselves, the one constant in the household was Analisa, a blonde-headed girl perhaps in late teens, who resembled an overgrown puppy dog with her bouncy manner and affectionate impulses. Ronnie explained to Melanie, the first time they were on their own, that back in stuffy old England Analisa would be treated as a servant, pure and simple; but amongst the Danish middle classes things were different. Okay, the girl had her round of duties, practically kept house for the Larson family; yet she was treated as an equal. sitting down to eat with Ola and Mariett and their guests.

The Larson home had an atmosphere of calm and relaxation that immediately endeared itself to Melanie. The large kitchen was the focus. There the coffee pot seemed always to be chugging away, while an ancient Telefunken radiogram in its walnut cabinet filled the lower reaches of the house with the ballads of Ray Charles and the saxophone of Charlie Parker.

Melanie woke to her first morning in the house, emerging from under the bulky duvet - something new to her, a duvet - with a guilty start. What had finally woken her? Was it the sidling up aroma of fried bacon? Quite possibly; but just as possible it was the girl, Analisa tickling Melanie under her chin and beaming down her sunburst of a smile.

"Hello there Miss Sleeping Beauty! Wakey, wakey now. I've brought you a nice cup of coffee."

Coming awake by inches, Melanie yawned and stretched. Then the realisation, the reason for that prick of guilt. "Oh my God, what time is it? I should be with Ronnie!"

"Ronnie said not to disturb, to let you sleep. I think you had a long day yesterday - no?" Giggling, Analisa held the coffee cup to Melanie's lips, allowing her a sip before removing the cup to the dresser. "Yes, your Ronnie has left for her business in the city. She says to me she will not need of you till tomorrow. Now do you dress in your mini that I like so much, or something else? Perhaps I show you into the shower first?"

Showered and dressed, Melanie skipped down to the hall to find Analisa waiting for her. "We go to the bakery now to fetch the bread and eat a croissant, if you would like?"

After lingering over their croissant and hot chocolate, they returned to the House to find Mariett laying places for - was it really lunchtime already? Ola was sat in a corner of the kitchen deep in his newspaper, while Neills, introduced to Melanie as "Our first-born," appeared to be sanding down a mechanical component of some sort. In the background the Telefunken played softly to itself.

Ola shoved aside his newspaper and stood to greet the girls. "So, you slept well I think? And now you have seen something of our neighbourhood." He waved Melanie to a seat at the table, sitting down opposite her, while Analisa flung on an apron and joined Mariett at the business end of the room. Noticing Melanie's interest in the radiogram, Ola asked, "This is your kind of music perhaps?"

"Oh gosh yes! Not the Jazz so much, but Soul, Soul I love, that and Irish Folk."

"Do you know, that radio has sat there for a quarter of a century. It was the very first thing my parents bought after the war. We had to wait, to save up for tables and chairs; the wireless, and most of all music, that came first."

Neills chipped in from the other end of the kitchen, "Watch out, Melanie, that's our Dad's cue; next he'll be telling you all about the Occupation and illegal use of cat's whisker radios."

Ola smiled. "No, no. We don't talk about those days any longer, apart from BBC. Your BBC was our North Star, our nightly drum beat of hope. Your BBC kept truth alive for the occupied nations. My young friends and I would hide away in our attics, willing those magic words, 'This is London' to come again out of the ether. And still today, Mariett will tell you, I like to listen to BBC World Service or drop off to the strains of Lily Bolero."

Neills looked up from his sanding. "It's true, most of us Danes love you English people, even when you make fools of yourselves with your moral posturing over the call-girl and the government minister. I think, I know we would want to have you closer to the new Europe."

"I agree with my son," Ola was fiddling with his cutlery, squaring the pieces into place. "Those old rivals, Germany and France showed us all the way with coal and steel leading to the common market which your country should be part of. We should have free access to your Bentleys and your Rolls Royces; you should welcome our fine Danish bacon, our superb Danish butter. We thought that the French had said *Non* to you joining in with a united states of Europe, but now it seems that Monsieur Pompidou may be having second thoughts. Anyway, I do hope so."

....

Two days went by during which Ronnie kept her Personal Assistant close to her. Negotiations at the top of the tower that overlooked Copenhagen's ancient harbour proved business-like but not without humour and a marked urbanity, characterised by tact and propriety. Discussions were in the English language. While she kept her head focused on her notepad, Melanie was absorbed by it all, and put up with the aching of her wrists at the close of each session.

On their last full day in the Danish capital, Ronnie confided to Melanie, "Tonight my dear, I've accepted an invitation to a meal and some relaxation out in the countryside. Ola and Mariett have an old friend, Peta, who has livery stables between here and Elsinore - you know, Hamlet's Elsinore - and we're invited to a venison supper. Analisa's coming; in fact, she'll be driving us there and back."

The three women set off early to avoid the worst of Copenhagen's evening traffic. The skies had a leaden look to them, and Melanie thought she could see a storm tracking over from the east; yet their spirits were high with the relaxation that comes from completing an important job of work.

"Just the evening for a bit of *Hygge*," Ronnie half turned from the front passenger seat.

"A bit of what?" Melanie queried.

"*Hygge*. We Brits don't know about *Hygge*, let alone how to pronounce the word, but it's great fun, isn't it Analisa? Tell me, Analisa, if I'm describing it wrongly, but *Hygge*'s deeply rooted in the Danish psyche. It's a warm atmosphere; you take time in your everyday life to slow down and enjoy the little things together with family and friends. Trust and a sense of security. Often enjoyed at home, but also at a casual meeting for a beer or a coffee and cake. No high-brow conversation, just happy chatting, no competition, no formal meals! Simplicity, fun. Danish winters are long and dark, so lots of candles and sitting in front of the fire. An escape from all that's wrong in the world."

From the driver's seat Analisa laughed unrestrainedly. "Yes my Ronnie, that is Danish *Hygge*. Great fun, great fun!"

"A word to the wise, my dear," Ronnie was turning back to Melanie. "Our hostess Peta is not married, but she has a little boy, still a baby, I believe. It was never on the cards that she would want to marry or even live with a man; she just wanted a child. No doubt his first real birthday present will be a saddle, eh Analisa?"

Peta's house, it turned out, was dominated by its stabling, so that they were greeted by the neighs and whinnies of horses poking heads out of stalls either side of the tack room.

The house itself, really one large room merging kitchen with living space, seemed to Melanie to have a wraparound feel to it, thanks to the blaze of log fire at one end and the thickness of the fur rugs scattered around the floor. Bubble and savour of venison stew cooked in alcohol of some sort blended with the resinous perfume of candles of which there were many, standing purple and proud around the walls.

Peta's greeting was as warm as her house. Bumper glasses of red wine were handed around between judicious tastings of the stew and chatter about the children's riding school which she was planning to open. The chat was in a mixture of Danish and English, but most of it Melanie was able to follow without too much difficulty.

They ate, sitting on stools at the breakfast bar. Steeped in its rich juices, the venison reminded Melanie of nothing she had ever tasted before. Crusty fresh bread layered with unsalted butter accompanied the stew.

After the meal Peta offered round thimble glasses of aquavit which took Melanie's breath away at the first sniffing. What was that her father had once told her? Something about not mixing the barley and the grape? Was it indeed barley? Melanie had no idea. Cocooned in the mounting warmth of the room and the waves of friendship all around her, she yet knew she should take it slowly, so she tucked her glass behind a convenient aspidistra, only to retrieve it minutes later.

Along with the fiery spirit there came toasts. They toasted Hans Christian Anderson followed by exotic-sounding figures of Danish folklore. Not wanting to be left out, Melanie chipped in with William Shakespeare before the round was completed by Danish and British royalties. Somewhere in the background the music of a folk group drifted soothingly to the ear.

After this and the laughter accompanying the toast-giving, the party seemed to lapse in on itself. Melanie found she was fighting to remain conscious. Out of drooping eyelids she saw Analisa get to her feet, weaving towards her, back-lit by the fire. The last thing she saw before wandering into unconsciousness was Ronnie and Peta coiled together in the big armchair, limbs awry, mouth to rosy mouth.

Mr Pym Goes to the Theatre

Winston Pym settled himself comfortably into his seat, focusing on the local dramatic society's programme for *Brigadoon* the musical. On either side of him sat his sister's grandchildren, Alice aged ten and Spencer seven. Treating the children to outings like this was as much a treat for Winston as it was for Alice and Spencer, but Winston fervently hoped that the youngsters would enjoy the production as much as he knew he would himself. Indeed he had been to the show the previous night, so he knew there was nothing about it that was likely to distress young minds and thus bring down his sister's wrath on his silver head. Set in the Highlands of Scotland and featuring a fairytale village that comes alive once in every hundred years, the plot included the obligatory love story which he thought would appeal to Alice, along with a sword dance which ought to be just the thing for Spencer. He had no concerns about gender ordering.

Born scarce weeks into the new century, Winston lived where he had always lived, in the village of Deering, in the Old Parsonage to be precise. He was a bachelor. All those years ago he had been engaged to Lily, a girl from the local tennis club. Lily had died. Possessed of a masterful back-hand return of service, at one moment she had shone with health and energy; within 48 hours she had succumbed to the virus scourging her generation, later to be known as the Spanish Flu. This had happened bare weeks after Winston's return from the trenches of the Great War in which he had just been old enough to be in at the crossing of the Sambre Canal. After Lily he had never seemed to have the heart to court another girl.

For his profession, Winston had followed his father to be the third generation of Pyms to head the family law firm. Week by week, year by year, bowler-hatted and sporting umbrella, briefcase and *Times* newspaper, he took the 7.50 up to town, striding from the terminus to his office in High Holborn. Going right back to the days when he had been articled to his father, the office had hummed with activity. In those days there had been four partners, a number of clerks and a lively bevy of stenographers. Gradually over the years, hastened by the privations of a second world war, the firm had shrunk to the point where now Winston had just the one ageing clerk and the one female typist, as they were now called.

As for business, gone were the halcyon days of large corporate fees. Those get-up-and-go Young Turks of yesteryear had got up and left the practice, preferring younger more dynamic blood to facilitate their road houses and ribbon developments, not that Winston minded too much. He still had a steady trickle of clients from the old days who clung to him and his practice like ivy clinging to a wall. Typical of these was Miss Bosenquet from Cheltenham. Despite having little to leave to her favoured animal charities, Miss Bosenquet was disciplined about reviewing the terms of her will and testament. Each year in January and July she went through the routine of making an appointment before travelling to town aboard the through train to Paddington, descending, refreshed by eau-de-Cologne, on High Holborn. The business of adding a codicil to her will in order to include a new charitable beneficiary was easily and promptly dealt with; what took rather longer beside making her day for her, was the chat with dear Mr Pym to reminisce about the "Good old days" before the war when it had still been possible to find a servant or live-in companion. Invariably these sessions were accompanied by Earl Grey tea served in the best Worcester bone china cups and saucers which Miss Bosenquet savoured all the way home to Cheltenham. If Winston bothered to send Miss Bosenquet a bill, this was never based on the time devoted to their meeting.

Then there was Klaus, an Austrian Jew and another regular at the offices of Cornish Pym & co. Klaus had fought against the Russians in the Great War before seeking asylum on Albion's fair shores. He was an inventor, perhaps more accurately a frustrated inventor of many things mechanical, relying on his old friend Winston to liaise with the Patents Office. Of late, Klaus had been working excitedly on a new method of desalination, sadly destined like many earlier inventions to fall short of the exacting standards required to achieve a patent. In common with most of Winston's clients, Klaus took up large swathes of solicitor time in exchange for modest fee return. The trouble was that Winston genuinely liked the Klauses and the Miss Bosenquets of his world, and would miss them sorely were they ever to cease consulting him. When the time finally came for retirement, he dreaded to think what there would be left for him to do, apart from completing his monograph on the canals of Northern France, on which he had embarked twenty years or more ago. This explained why the occasional outing with young Alice and Spencer meant so much to Winston.

The orchestra struck up the overture with a fine flourish while buzz of conversation through the packed audience died away. The children fidgeted in their seats with anticipation, each tucking a slim hand into Winston's.

As the fanciful tale unwound, Winston found his eyes were misting over whenever the lovers went roaming in the heather. To distract himself from thoughts of a wistful kind and at some point well into the performance, he got to studying the chorus line. One young woman in particular caught and kept his attention. This girl - Winston thought she could barely be out of her teens - had the most striking auburn hair framing the freckled pallor of her beautiful young face. She was so animated, so focused on what she was doing that it shone out across the footlights, while her dance movements seemed to pull the rest of the chorus along as if on invisible strings.

The interval arrived; the house lights went up. After shepherding Alice and Spencer to the toilets and back before indulging them with strawberry ices, Winston settled back down to have a closer scrutiny of his programme. Going through the names of the chorus to see if he could identify Miss Auburn-hair, he came up with a start. If his deductions were right then she had to be a Miss Mel Mulligan, and that name he was sure he knew.

It finally came to Winston just as the orchestra was building up to its finale. The name Mulligan was boldly printed across a large manilla envelope that lay at that moment in the recesses of his office safe, the old Chub, receptacle for so many secrets over the years. Of course it could be a coincidence; there might be other Mulligans out there, though the initial M went some way towards shortening the odds. And then he had it. The bulky envelope had been addressed and also secured with sealing wax by none other than his village neighbour Blane Farley. It had been over a year ago, yet Winston recalled the occasion clearly. Blane Farley had come to Winston's office by appointment and with the intention of signing the will prepared for him by Winston himself. In the event Farley had decided against signing the will, confiding to Winston that he needed more time to consider what he termed, "Some finer points." But while he was there, Farley had produced his envelope, asking for the loan of the lawyer's sealing wax. The wording added to the face of the envelope now came back to Winston. Farley had written, "In the event of my death or loss of mental capacity, this envelope is to be delivered PERSONALLY to Miss M. Mulligan, strictly in the offices of Messrs Cornish Pym & co." "PERSONALLY" was written in bold, yet Winston had been given no address for Miss M. Mulligan, and no means by which he might contact the lady. In the meantime Blane Farley had died. Indeed, Winston had made a point of attending the funeral at Deering's

Parish Church. After a few days of silence for propriety's sake, he had spoken with the widow to explain that her husband had not returned to sign the will and that, as a result, his client could have died intestate. Winston omitted to say anything about the envelope secured in the firm's safe as to do that would, in his eyes, have been a gross breach of trust.

Now Winston was in a dilemma. He knew this was his chance to carry out his client's instruction by seeking out the auburn-haired girl and testing her connection, if any, with Blane Farley; yet the thought of invading a dressing-room seething with young bodies, possibly half naked, filled him with trepidation, besides which there were the children to think about.

Winston was not well equipped to deal with the situation with no cards or letterheads to hand. The best he could do was to turn his theatre programme inside out, and write a message which he addressed to "Miss M. Mulligan," briefly explaining who he was and requesting that she should meet him at the stage door to learn something to her advantage. Alice and Spencer trailing behind, he tracked down the door he thought he wanted, just as a youngster - he could have been part of *Brigadoon*'s chorus - burst out in front of him. The message changed hands, the assignment speeded by a half crown tip.

Winston then stood back from the door, all too well aware of Alice and Spencer shivering at his side. Tapping his foot impatiently he stood on the spot for a good ten minutes, at which point he promised himself he would wait no more than another five. The five minutes went by. The stage door remained stubbornly closed. He turned about, shepherding his charges back to his car.

Ralph is Restless

Term was winding down. Students strolled or lay about the campus lawns, transistor radios blasting out the Top Twenty. Last essays were scooped out of pigeonholes by frazzled tutors and borne off to lonely rooms. Ralph Ransom was one such tutor, wishing that he had more appetite for the derivative efforts to illuminate the National Parliament of the French Revolution.

He slumped to his bed and selected the first essay in the pile. This was authored by one of his more conscientious students, a young woman who was certain to end up with a respectable Lower Second degree. What a pity it was that she managed little more than to parrot his lecture notes back at him. The reading took no time at all. Below the tick Ralph wrote, "Next time try harder to think yourself into the topic."

Then there turned up a rather different treatment by a more lateral thinking student, name of Sebastian. This time there was no parroting of Ralph's notes, more evidence of originality despite careless use of sources. He was about to award a tick with a question mark when he uncovered an additional page. This page contained a scrawl of pencilled notes evidently taken from Ralph's lectures. His first thought was that Sebastian had carelessly bundled the notes up with the essay, but then he had to think again as he took in the heading, "F.M.'s notes." As there was no one in the department with the initials "F.M." Ralph had to deduce he himself was "F.M.," and that this was short for "Frankenstein's Monster." On balance it was likely that the inclusion of the notes was no moment of carelessness, but a small act of cruelty. Was he, he wondered, "F.M." or even "Frank" to the whole of the department?

He tossed Sebastian aside and lay back on the bed. Morosely, he was debating with himself whether to tackle more of the essay pile when a knock came at the door and Mrs Burton edged into the room. Mrs Burton was the cleaner assigned to Ralph's block in the hall of residence. Small, neat of movement, she was one of those women to whom it was hard to put an age. Ralph's guess would have been 40. Because he occasionally exchanged greetings with her, Ralph knew she had come to England from the Caribbean as a girl, and that she had several children. He knew the last bit because Mrs Burton could often be heard complaining, "If it weren't for those kiddies, I's wouldn't need to slave away like this all hours the good Lord sends!"

Ralph propped himself on an elbow, ready to ask the woman whether she would not mind coming back later. Mrs Burton got in first. With a smile as broad as her face and a wag of her finger, she looked straight at Ralph. "Now then, Mr Ransom Sir, you a terrible man, you about to tell me to come back later - no?"

"Well, Mrs Burton …"

"Only I's can't do that, you see, cos we'm all behind hand today." This with a slosh of the mop in her bucket.

For several seconds Ralph stared at the woman, seeing her as if for the first time, taking in the dimpled arms, the beguiling sway of the nubile hips. The need for a woman stabbed at the core of him. The last time had so nearly been with barmaid Rita. An image of Rita arching backwards to undo something flickered across Ralph's brain, only to be replaced by the nightmarish vision of the burning corpse she so nearly had been.

Coming out of his reverie he laughed, "Okay, okay, you win, Mrs B! I'm out of here!" He loped from the room, leaning his body away from the gaze of the cleaner.

....

Ralph knew only that he had to get away from the campus. His first thought was Kate. Kate would put him up for a week without thinking twice. He greatly admired the way she had coped with losing Blane, besides which she was still very dear to him. Their jaunt across the Channel to Paris had proved to be a breath of fresh air for them both. The only problem was, Kate felt sorry for him, and pity was something Ralph had yet to deal with. Physically she attracted him; maybe she loved him a little; yet that love was a mother's for a wounded soldier of a son. Gritting his teeth at the thought, Ralph decided instead to "Get it over with," the "It" being reunion with family.

The countryside of Royal Berkshire was smiling as Ralph wound through the lanes and down the long drive to Tudors, scorching to a halt midst a fine spray of gravel.

He and Beatrice had met up just the twice since Ralph's accident, and each time more or less in passing. Despite an interrupted year of nurse's training, his mother was not good with emergencies and their emotional consequences. When Ralph's father had been carried in from the hunting field, much more dead than alive, Beatrice had simply wrung her hands, leaving it to the Master of Hounds to call for an ambulance and to rally the family.

Now Beatrice stayed sitting in her armchair in the drawing room while her eldest son marched in, a weak effort at a smile momentarily softening his face. "Please forgive me not getting up, the old rheumatics are particularly bad today. Have you come to stay, or is this simply a flying visit?" This with a slight but discernible emphasis on the last two words.

Ralph slung down his travelling bag and stared at his mother. "Don't know yet, Ma. Anyway, give me a moment to freshen up and I'll be with you. May I bring you in a cup of something?"

"Thank you, Dear. I'll have my usual tea."

Five minutes and Ralph was back, balancing a silver tray bearing Earl Grey tea in his mother's favourite Rockingham china. He slumped to the settee. "The roses are looking good, Ma."

Beatrice kept her eyes down on her embroidery. "Oh yes, they're having a decent enough year, though old Dent still does his best to kill them. If I've told him once I've told him a hundred times, you don't need to prune them back to the Stone Ages!" She took a cautious sip of her tea. "Thank you, Ralph, a little more milk would have been nice."

"How are Philip and the girls?"

"They're fine, as far as I know. The girls are all busy, busy, busy. They won't want to see you, but Philip might. He did ask after you the last time we spoke. He seems to lead a rather insular life despite living and working in the Big City. You could do worse than to look him up on your travels."

Ralph drew a big breath before asking, "So Mother, how do you think I'm looking now?"

Beatrice glanced up from her lap momentarily, then down again at her cross stitch. "You look, you sound, well, a little better in yourself. You had a frightful, a terrible, accident. It will take us all time to get over it. Had either of you actually died, I mean, had you died in company with that barmaid, it would have been worse than, than going to hospital in week-old underwear!"

Ralph raised his eyes to the ceiling and chewed on a lip while his mother launched into her stride. "I really don't know what you're doing at your age, cavorting around the countryside with barmaids in tow. When you think, you've had so many chances to marry, to settle down with the right sort of gal. Let's see now, there was that nice little thing, sister of your Eton friend,

Victoria, I think she was. Then there was Bubbles Beatty from the Hunt - she certainly had an eye for you. Oh yes and dear Freddie, your cousin Freddie, - she'd have passed muster. Then there's ..."

"Wo wo, hang on there, Ma. First I've no idea who Victoria might have been. As for Freddie, Freddie was last heard of cooling her heels in a Casablanca jail accused of something to do with drug-running. Then you say Bubbles? Well she never had her eye on me. Bubbles likes women! And before you mention grandchildren, you can hardly need reminding the girls are busy producing the best part of a Hockey team!" Ralph sprang to his feet. "Anyway, I'm off to take a turn around the park. Enjoy your tea."

....

Philip's antiquarian book shop was on Frith Street in the heart of London's Soho, not far from Ronnie Scott's Jazz Club.

Ralph was glad he had not attempted to drive up to town, preferring to leave his car at Tudors. Apart from the horrors of finding somewhere to park, he found nothing threatening about trains where he could hide himself behind his newspaper. The streets of the capital were equally anonymous for the simple reason that no one spared a look in your direction.

While Philip brewed coffee, Ralph toured the toppling shelves of his brother's stock-in-trade, lifting down the odd volume or two that caught his eye. With each book there followed a fine showering of dust. While he browsed, not a single customer found their way to the first floor premises, nor did any telephone bell break the tomb-like silence.

Sat down with coffee, Ralph enquired of his brother, "How on earth do you make a living, you and your partner?"

"Ah well you see, Dennis doesn't have to worry about that - born with the silver spoon, don't you know. He operates like the gentleman farmer, except in his case it's the gentleman purveyor of books on rare birds. Hardly ever see him, actually. As for me, I do a pretty steady trade in antiquaries, first editions and so on."

"So there's money in that?"

"Oh yes, you bet! The secret is knowing your customer and knowing where to source what the customer has been yearning to possess. I am, if you like, the bridge, in vulgar parlance, the fixer. Right now, for example, I have on my books a dear old boy, a literary tutor of some sort, who has been hankering after an early Emily Dickinson first edition for years. It so happens I've just tracked down exactly what he's been searching for. Are you a fan of the Bard of Amherst?"

"Can't say I am, no."

"Okay, so Emily was nineteenth century, 1830 something to 1880 something. Lived in the small town of Amherst in Massachusetts; bit of a recluse, living much of her life in her bedroom; dressing habitually in white; yet a truly prolific writer of verse. Much of her work was collected and edited as late as the 1950s, some of her early stuff was published in limited edition during her lifetime, and it's one of those first editions that I've managed to track down for my client."

"How do you know it's the genuine article?"

"We veterans of the trade know by instinct how to trust each other, or not, as the case may be, and I know who I'm dealing with in this case. Besides which, I've had photographs from over the Pond. Only trouble is, understandably they want to exchange merchandise for banker's draft, and in person, and just at the moment I'm reluctant to leave the shop." Philip paused to swallow the rest of his coffee. "Ralph Old Man, I don't suppose …"

"I'd be willing to do the courier thing?"

"Well, it's a thought - always supposing you've got the time. Apart from the money side of things, there's no way I would risk that manuscript in the post. So yes, what about it? You could fly stand-by and back for next to nothing, and obviously I'll give you your expenses plus a bonus up front. Just need to fish out those photographs and go through some routine authentication rules with you."

"All right then, Bro. You're on. Give me time to retrieve the old passport, and I'll be on my way. Why don't you check with your chums in Boston that we can meet up, say, Friday of next week?"

Later the brothers dined together on Charlotte Street. Over the coffee and brandy Ralph ventured, "This must be the first time we've seen each other since my accident."

"Actually no, Ralph. I peeped in on you at the hospital after your first operation."

"Oh right. More than Ma or any of the girls managed then!"

"Realise Ralph, you weren't a pretty sight back then. I reckon you're getting there now, and Ralph," Philip drained his brandy with a flourish. "I think you've changed, it's changed you."

A Message from Blane

As usual, it took Melanie ages to remove her makeup and moisturise her fair skin. The process called for concentration with the rest of the chorus competing for mirror space and generally jostling around. Finally she was done. She was zipping her theatre bag when she noticed a discarded programme sheet cluttering up the desk. Melanie was in the act of consigning the programme to the bin when she happened to glance at the sheet, and spotted her name. Closer inspection and she saw there was something that looked like a message, "Cornish Pym Solicitors" and "Something to your advantage." The programme went into her bag.

Back at work the following day, Melanie showed the message to Ronnie, who assured her, "No, my dear, I don't believe it's a practical joke. We know Cornish Pym & co., they've been around since Adam was a lad. Highly respectable practice. Why don't you take a long lunch and look them up?"

The man who greeted Melanie had owlish eyes behind large tortoiseshell glasses, an ivory cast of face, and rounded shoulders. "Come through, come through. I'm Pym, Winston Pym, and I'm the chap whose scribbled note has brought you to our door. Can't tell you how much I enjoyed the show, by the way. I imagine you must have another couple of nights to go, yes?"

Not having been in a solicitor's office before, Melanie looked about her with a mixture of diffidence and curiosity. There was a smell to the place as if ancient dust from the Blitz continued to trickle from the eves. "It was only by the merest chance that I got your note, Mr Pym. I haven't been able to think of much else since."

"Now, young lady, I'm going to take you in to what we still grandly call our conference room, sit you down with a cup of something, and leave you to it while you examine the contents of a certain envelope that has been in our safe custody for a while now. But first, may I trouble you to give me your full name, your current address, and what you can tell me about the village of Deering."

Satisfied with the girl's responses, the solicitor closed the door of the Conference Room with the quietest of clicks, while Melanie slit open the envelope with the silver sword provided. One glance at the handwriting she withdrew from the envelope confirmed what she had half been expecting, what she had secretly been hoping for. She read:-

My Darlingest Girl,

I hope you will forgive me for the cloak and dagger, but sometimes it's easier to jot things down than it is to say them out loud. You always twitted me about disguise of the emotions, and of course, as ever, you were right.

Truth is, Old Girl, I haven't been feeling so chipper just of late. Remember my huff and puff when we tried a bit of our friendly Austrian mountain! So, I didn't want to leave it to chance to tell you what you have meant, what you mean to me, and also to do something practical for my Darling, should the worst come to the worst.

Only redeemed by our coming together in that blessed Corner House, my life has dwindled down to disappointment. I know that I have a loyal wife; I have two children of whom I am rightly proud; yet a Chap always needs to have horizons, and mine, I'm afraid, have closed in on me. My North Star has dimmed to a distant glow.

In earlier days, things were different. Eton did me proud, Eton, you could say, made me. Then, returning from Korea, complete with battle scars, I was, if you like, the Man of the moment, feted by all, courted by many.

For a time, marriage and later on fatherhood bore me along on the crest of a wave. Okay, I had no degrees, no qualifications of any sort apart from expertise in siting artillery and killing the enemy; yet in those days I was optimistic. Starting out, I tried my luck with the big corporations, but I didn't like them and they didn't like me. I then went into partnership with a fellow ex-officer from the Gloucesters. Our business was selling double glazed units to housewives averse to draughts. The business prospered. I did most of the up-front salesmanship myself, having - as my partner put it - "Something of a way with the ladies." But that was until, with the help of my accountant, I found I was being cheated by my partner who had been creaming off the top line and living the high life while leaving it to me to do the leg-work. The Inland Revenue got involved as a major creditor and, to cut a sorry story short, the business went bust.

As you may imagine, my Love, this experience brought me down with a bang. In the short term we had nothing to live on other than my Army pension and Kate's part-time teaching. But it cast a longer, a deeper shadow by stripping away my confidence. In place of dash and doing, I found I was living by caution, imagining big battalions waiting in ambush over the hill, rather like one of my heroes, "Little Mac," of whom I might write separately.

But Mel, this mustn't be all about me. You are the one who matters. With your youth and those amazing looks, you have your whole life in front of you, not forgetting that rainbow we talked about! So what I'm saying is, I can't bear to think of you being cast adrift, so to speak. While I have every reason to believe that you would make your own way, I want you to have a couple of things of greater practical use than this maudlin epistle.

The first - and please don't feel insulted, Dear - is a few pennies to rub together, to tide you over, just in case that should be necessary. The fact that you are reading this letter is enough to have old Pym unlock the cash box. The other thing, the more important, is a name. Perhaps it's been my fault for sweeping you into my exclusive world, but you've never seemed to be flush with friends to turn to. Ralph - I'm printing his home address overleaf - is a true friend. He and I have been chums ever since he fagged for me at the old school, after which he gained a commission in the Guards. In other words, he's a stout chap and, by the by, dashed good looking into the bargain, quite a latter day Rupert Brooke in fact, as well as a bachelor to boot. So, my Dear, if you're ever needing help, just look up Ralph Ransom, oh and don't forget to give him salutations from his friend and brother officer.

"Anyway, I think I've gone on long enough. Let's hope and pray that one day we will stroll over Westminster Bridge together, making confetti of these pages and chucking them into the Thames. If not then all I can say to my Playgirl, my Darling Mel, is I love you, and I thank you from the bottom of my heart for the happiness you have brought me. Farewell my beautiful one, farewell." And the letter was signed "Ever your loving Playboy Blane".

Through a swell of hot tears Melanie noticed that there was indeed a final page. With only half her attention, in need as she was of reading the letter again, she briefly took in that Blane had jotted down some notes possibly for a future book. The notes appeared to centre on the conduct of a certain Major General George Brinton McClellan, Commander of Union forces in the early stages of the American Civil War. The notes suggested that McClellan had won battles against the Confederates, that he had been lionised by the grand ladies of Washington, but had later thrown away advantages through over caution, repeatedly over-estimating the strength of the enemy. The final note had a double question mark to it, and read, "Would the war have ended two years earlier had Grant commanded in place of McClellan, thus limiting the actual and eventual death toll of six hundred and sixty thousand men??"

Melanie walked out of the offices of Cornish Pym & co. in a daze. Hardly knowing where she was going, she walked two blocks south and found an empty bench in the sunshine of Lincoln's Inn Fields. A pair of monks in saffron robes were walking backwards and forwards in earnest conversation, while behind Melanie's bench a grandmotherly figure was explaining to her grandson why they did not have time to visit Hamley's. Melanie had no awareness of any of it.

After slowly rereading Blane's letter, Melanie found her mind was wandering to the strange sequence of events that had led to that day's revelations. She supposed it had all started with Ronnie. After sweeping her out of the typing pool in bizarre fashion, it had been Ronnie who had instilled in her the confidence to join - not the Royal Court exactly - but an amateur dramatic society that now felt something like a family. That had led to the amazing coincidence of Winston Pym happening to be at the show and to recognise her name in the programme. Then finally there had been the chance that had drawn her eye to the message so nearly discarded. Was it all coincidence, Melanie wondered, or was it in some way meant, the breadcrumb trail to the magical house in the woods.

A fat pigeon flopped to the rail of the bench, but flapped away as soon as it spied no food in the offing. Melanie sat on a further 15 minutes before coming back to life with a start. As she headed back for the Department the thought idly lapped her mind, "If she was meant to find her Blane again, then perhaps she was meant to find Blane's friend."

Melanie and Beatrice

Flush with the funds meticulously counted out by Mr Pym and duly signed for, Melanie decided on something she had never in her life done before, she ordered a taxi, a taxi from Slough station. Stretching back in the passenger seat she told herself, "No, Melanie, you are not nervous," this with a glance to her tights to check there were no ruckles. Her sage green pinafore dress, cream blouse and belted camelhair coat all added to her feeling of self-confidence.

Arrived at Tudors, a crag of a house, she was uncertain whether or not to dismiss the taxi. There had been no means of telegraphing her impromptu visit, so it followed that she was not expected. A prick of doubt hit Melanie. It was the weekend, so it was unlikely that Blane's friend would be at work; all the same, he might be anywhere other than home, in which case she would have to turn tail, telling herself what a fool she was.

Once she had tried the doorbell twice without response, the drumming of her driver's hands on the steering wheel reminded her she had to come to a decision. She was turning to get back in the taxi when, out of the corner of her eye, she spotted movement some way off. Impulsively she thrust the fare into the cabby's hand, thanked him and sent him on his way.

Rounding the gable of the house, there shambled into view a stick of a man, pushing a wheelbarrow. "Can us help you, Miss? I'm Dent her Ladyship's gardener by the way."

Melanie took a few steps towards the man. "I'm Melanie Mulligan and I was hoping to find Ralph Ransom at home, but there's no reply to the bell."

"Well," Dent dropped his barrow and straightened his back. "Suppose you could see her Ladyship. Mind you, she'll be in her chicken coat you know."

"Sorry, chicken coat? What might that be?"

The gardener assumed a quizzical expression as much as to say, "Townies eh?" "Of course, the coat her puts on to feed the chucks. Always tell her I'll be happy to do it, but her Ladyship don't trust me, thinks I'll give them too much to eat, you knows."

"If there's no one else at home, perhaps I could see Mrs Ransom?"

"Don't know whether she'll want to see you in her chicken coat." He was again lifting the barrow.

With a note of desperation Melanie came back with, "Please, I must, I would like to see Mrs, I mean Lady Ransom. Can you show me round to, to the chickens perhaps?"

The gardener was knuckling his chin, indecision creasing his gnarled face when his employer - Melanie intuited it could only be "Her Ladyship" - emerged out of nowhere. "Young lady, you look lost. Can we give you directions?"

Melanie turned to see a woman, perhaps 60, but a well preserved 60, with greying hair gathered back in a bun. The chicken coat could not be anything other than a coat in which to feed the chickens; yet it was not the coat that held the eye, much more the classically moulded cheek bones. "My name is Melanie, Melanie Mulligan, and I've called on the off chance of seeing Ralph Ransom. You see, I've got an important message for him from an old friend."

While Dent the gardener ambled away with his barrow, Beatrice Ransom considered her visitor. "I'm afraid my son is not at home just now. Sorry to disappoint you. I don't see a car, so how have you got here?"

"I came by taxi from the railway station, but he's gone back now."

Beatrice continued to study Melanie, employing the art of those who can price each and every item of the other woman's ensemble, without appearing to stare. "You poor thing. Tell you what, I'm ready for my tea, so come along and join me, why don't you? Then we can see about getting you back to town." As she spoke she led the way into the house. "Kitchen's that away," pointing down a discrete corridor. "Why don't you put the kettle on while I get out of these old things."

Obediently Melanie found her way to the kitchen, located an electric kettle lurking on a shelf, filled it with water and switched it on. Not wanting to exceed her brief, she wandered back to the hall. There was no sign of Lady Ransom so she looked in at an open doorway, the door clearly to the drawing room. Had she known it, Melanie was looking at "old money," furniture and furnishings slightly distressed while elegantly disposed. Yet what drew her eye to the far end of the room was a portrait of the Madonna With Child, subtly lit and set in blue enamel.

Melanie started as the chatelaine of Tudors materialised at her side. "Oh gosh, I'm sorry, I wasn't really being nosey," she managed to stammer out.

"No Dear, of course you weren't. Now come along and we'll have our tea."

In the kitchen Lady Ransom resumed, "Suggest you have that chair - less likely to get dog hairs on that nice dress."

Melanie duly sat while her hostess busied herself with the tea-making. "It's the maid's day off, you realise. Do I detect a little bit of the Irish in my visitor?"

Momentarily thrown by the abrupt segway, Melanie could only stammer out, "My Dad was from County Sligo, but how? ..."

Beatrice Ransom poured the tea into mugs and sat herself down as a Jack Russell terrier launched across the room with the air of a proprietor. "Ah well now, I spotted you admiring Our Lady, that and the way your complexion so compliments your lovely green dress. Anyway, who is this friend who wishes to be remembered to my son." And then, half rising from her chair, "Fergus! You naughty, naughty boy! Our guest does not want you ravishing her nice new tights, does she?" At which the hound turned tail and slunk away to the AGA range.

Melanie thought afterwards, she should have been ready for the question. A long sup of her tea and she replied, "They were at school together, though Blane was older," and she added, with the hint of a white lie, "And I believe they were in the army together."

"Would I know the Chap?"

"I don't think so."

"Ah well, I'll pass on what you've told me. Now, if you would care to, please tell me about yourself, yes?"

Lacking fluency, but maintaining eye contact for the most part, Melanie embarked upon an account of childhood, parents, the Civil Service, and her newly found love of singing and dancing in front of the footlights. The "parents" part, she managed carefully to sanitise. Towards the end of the saga, she found she was staring at a framed photograph of a youngish man that hung above the fridge. A prick of disappointment went through her. The face that gazed out of the portrait was by no means unpleasant; yet the thin lips and the receding chin were not quite what she had been imagining.

Beatrice reached for her embroidery. "Right, so your father came from over the water, did he? And have you lived over there at all?"

"No, I'm afraid not."

"I noticed you were looking at the photograph of my son. Not that we see very much of Philip these days."

"Your son Philip? I thought it must be Ralph, Ralph Ransom, no?"

"No, my Dear, that's my younger boy, Philip, into old books and that; has a shop in town. But I'll go and get you Ralph's photograph, if you would like."

Casting aside her embroidery, Beatrice got creakingly to her feet. While his mistress was out of the room, Fergus thought about another rush at the interloper in his kitchen, but decided better of it, preferring a vigorous scratch of his nether parts instead.

Beatrice returned, bearing a glossy eight-by-six framed portrait. Taking the frame between her hands, Melanie took in she was looking at a strong-jawed young man in uniform, the ghost of a smile flicking across the full face. "Ah, so this is Ralph?" Melanie handed the portrait back to avoid any suggestion of over eagerness.

"Yes, that's Number One Son, much younger then of course." And returning to her chair she added with a sigh, "Yes, two sons, no heir, no spare. Anyway, we'd better see about getting you back to town, hadn't we?"

"Thank you, Lady Ransom, and thank you for the tea. I'm sorry that I've missed Mr Ransom. Perhaps ..."

"Yes, Ralph only left for the States this morning and may be away for some time, but why don't you let me have your address, oh and I'll be sure to pass on your message."

....

Almost as soon as she entered her block, Melanie sensed there was someone on the landing, very possibly outside her own door. A wisp of familiar perfume hung on the heavy air of the hallway; yet the impatient tap tap of the foot was the real give-away. A flush of annoyance with herself for being out of town longer than intended bore her upwards to the first floor, and there was Keelie, shopping bags piled around her feet.

"Oh! So you've decided to come home, have you? Me, I was just about to leave, give you up as a no-show."

"Sorry sorry! I'm really sorry, Ma. I've been out to the country, didn't notice the time."

They were in the flat now, and Melanie's mother was emptying bags in Melanie's kitchen. "I promised I'd come round and make you a good filling meal - you're far too thin - so here I am."

"Well yes, Ma, but you made that promise months ago! Do you realise, this is the first time you've come to see me here?"

"I've been out of the country a lot, Rome, Paris, New York, one exhibition after another."

While her mother started in on some aggressive chopping and slicing, Melanie raced around her living room, plumping a cushion here and straightening a picture there. In mid-stride she noticed her miniature portrait of Blane in its leather carrying case. Her first instinct was to hide the photograph; then, for some reason, she drew her hand back, leaving Blane in pride of place on the mantelpiece.

"Say if you need help, Ma."

"No, I'm fine. Glass of wine would be nice though!"

By the time Melanie had wiped clean a couple of glasses and poured the wine, her mother was slamming the oven door and coming through to sit down. "Thank you, Dear. So here's to you! Tell me what you've been up to since I saw you last."

Melanie started on a recital of her progress through the Department. She was a little way into her Denmark trip when Keelie interrupted. "I notice you have no photos of your mother on view, but who may I ask is the older gentleman staring at me from the mantelpiece?"

Melanie looked up. "His name is Blane. He died some months ago."

"Oh my dear girl, were you and he? ..."

"Yes Ma, we were, we were lovers."

Keelie hastily rested her glass down and came to sit by Melanie on the settee, extending a hand towards her daughter. "You kept that very quiet. I had no idea. Do you want to tell me about it, or not?"

A long pause and then, head bowed, Melanie began haltingly to pick through her memories, not certain just how much her mother wanted or needed to hear. At the end she said, "I was all set to hide him from you, but I changed my mind. I'm not ashamed of Blane, of what we did, what we were. He taught me so much, so much about, well, life. We visited some special places. We looked to the beautiful heart of things, two pairs of eyes as one. I hadn't done that since, well ..."

"Since your father died," she paused, "Since I drove him to the bottle and pushed the two of you into an unholy alliance against, well, I suppose, against me."

Edward Makes a Discovery

Over the weeks since his brother-in-law's death, Edward Upchurch had wondered that he had not been told of any will. He had taxed Kate more than once with the question. Each time his sister had slid away from the subject, only to admit finally that "Dear old Pym" had failed to come up with anything, concluding that Blane had died intestate.

Now, Edward decided it really was his duty to visit Kate and find an opportunity to have a good poke around in the Den. He thought about asking Genevieve if she would like to accompany him, but then decided against the idea. He loved his mother as much as he loved Kate; but whenever the two women got together friction tended to break out between them after the first half hour. Besides which, Edward wanted his sister to himself. So it was that Edward arrived in Kate's village well before it was time for Kate to pick up Jane and Jack from school.

"You're looking well, Sister Dear!" Edward's greeting was upbeat.

Brother and sister moved through to the kitchen. Edward sat himself down at the table while Kate busied herself with making coffee. "Yes, Ed, I think I'm getting there."

"And what about my Niece and Nephew?"

Kate turned to pour the coffee. "Well, as you would expect, they have both been quite numbed, not able to understand why it has happened to them, to us. As you know, they adored their father even though he seemed to have less and less time to spend with them. Jack still gets his Meccano set out to puzzle over the model they were making together. As for Jane, well, you know my daughter, she's doing her best to come to terms with it in her own quite secretive way."

"Thanks Sis, yes, I will have one of those biscuits, if you're offering. I think you're telling me that Blane was something of a hero to the kids?"

"Blane was a good father. It wasn't Blane's fault that money became a problem, that he got sick, that he died."

Edward moved chairs to sit next to his sister. Reaching a hand out to Kate, he paused before saying, "No, Kate, some of that could have been down to me. You won't know this, but the day Blane died we'd had the mother and father of a row on the telephone. It's been on my mind ever since that it might have triggered his heart attack."

Kate stared at her brother for several seconds before, in a small voice she asked, "What were you rowing about?"

Edward looked away, pursing lips, evidently struggling with some deep down emotion. Finally he looked back at his sister. "I never wanted to tell you this, Kate, but I'm afraid your husband was not quite the paragon you seem to think he was." He paused. "You see, I'd found out something about, about his private life, something, well, pretty shaming. I hadn't really meant to confront him with this, but on that day he stung me with a little home truth of his own, and that was when I reacted, rather too pointedly I'm afraid."

A long silence as brother and sister stared at each other. "You're talking about Blane's mistress, you're talking about Mel, aren't you?" It was more of a statement than a question.

Edward looked as if he had been kicked in the stomach. "But how on earth, how ...?"

"How do I know? I found a letter in the Den, a letter from her. There were others."

Edward half rose, fists bunched. "No Ed, sit down. They're not there now, and things have moved on since then. Mel and I have met, met a couple of times in fact. Hard for you to believe perhaps, but she's a really nice kid." A further silence while Edward stared at his sister, his jaw working soundlessly. "And talking of kids, it's time I went to collect mine. We parents are invited to view Year Six's exhibition of artwork, so I'll be a little time." Kate got up, reaching for coat and hat. "We'll be as quick as we can. Just help yourself to anything you need."

The door had barely shut behind Kate when Edward was diving into the Den, where he found the filing cabinet unlocked. Well aware of his sister's lack of interest in matters legal, matters of business, he was curious to discover if there was anything hiding away, anything that might help Blane's family.

Edward struck gold almost at once. In a file, helpfully labelled "Insurances," he found a total of three policy documents. The motor insurance and the household insurance he scarcely looked at, save to check the expiry date in each case, and to make a note of this for when it came to renew cover. But the item that drew a big breath from Edward and got him sat down at the desk turned out to be a recent policy written by Sentinel Life Assurance co. of Leadenhall Street, London E.C., a policy written on the life of the Proposer, Blane Alexander Maxwell Farley.

Edward knew he was looking at a genuine and original policy document. He recognised the seal, he even recognised the director's signature having recently handled business with the company on behalf of a client. He approved of The Sentinel as it was one of the leading Mutual offices, belonging as it did to its members as opposed to shareholders.

Turning to the schedule Edward noted with an arching of his eyebrows that his brother-in-law had insured his life in the sum of £20,000, a hefty sum for the time. The policy was written under trust, the Trustees being Kate Elizabeth Farley and a certain Winston Pym of High Holborn. Under "Beneficiaries," Blane or someone had inserted, "My Wife Kate is to be regarded as my primary beneficiary, but my Trustees are to have the discretion set out in the accompanying Deed of Trust of even date herewith." How typical of Blane to complicate matters, Edward thought. He knew little about the intricacies of discretionary trusts, though he had often suspected they were a device invented by lawyers in order to make money for lawyers.

Unfortunately, however, there was no evading the caveat boldly set out on the face of the policy document. There ought to be little problem in getting Sentinel Life to pay out on the contract. Following Blane's death, bearing in mind his recent visit to Dr Price, there had been no need for a post-mortem, let alone an inquest. Production of a certified copy of the death certificate along with the policy document should suffice to release the funds. As the contract was "With profits," the pay-out could well exceed the basic sum insured. It would be for Kate and "Dear old Pym" to apply to Sentinel. Yet there was no ducking the need to track down that Trust Deed, as the professional in Edward reasoned ... But then he thought again. What if this mysterious deed contained something capable of diminishing his sister's inheritance?

....

The three of them sat around the conference table at the offices of Cornish Pym & co. Half of the table was bathed in bright sunlight, scintillating the green of the baize covering. The remaining half was in shadow.

Both Kate and Edward had dressed for the occasion. Kate was in the outfit she had worn for the funeral; Edward predictably was in suit and tie. Between the siblings, Winston Pym sat hunched over, wearing his most solemn of faces.

Kate introduced the two men to each other. In the solicitor's canon of propriety Edward Upchurch had no official status as he was not a party to the legal formalities; yet "Dear Kate" had wanted her brother to be present, and that was good enough for Pym.

Pym opened the meeting on what he hoped was a positive note by confirming that he had that day received Sentinel's cheque in payment of the policy proceeds. The settlement, he observed, was a most healthy one. Then, with a drawn out clearing of the throat, he reached for a paper. "As you would expect, as soon as I heard about this, hmm, deed of trust, I had a careful search made of all our securities here in the office. We found nothing. I therefore requested of Sentinel Life that they send me anything relevant from their file. What I am now going to read is what I was sent in response." He removed his spectacles giving them a quick rub before replacing them and starting to read.

To my Trustees:--

Clause one. Having disappointed you, Dear Kate, for so long in my role as provider, my ship has finally come in. I have landed a substantial advance on my next book, and this has paid for the premium to finance the insurance on my life. You, my Trustees, are therefore to treat my Wife, Kate Elizabeth Farley, as my primary beneficiary, subject only to the following discretionary requests.

Clause two. It is my dear wish that our son Jack should follow in my footsteps and in the footsteps of his grandfather by going to Eton College. I wish therefore that my Trustees consider establishing a trust fund with a view to financing Jack's education when the time comes for him to move on from his present school. I realise that this makes no account of our beloved daughter, Janie, but Janie is so bright I know she will succeed wherever further education takes her.

Clause three. Returning to the subject of my book, and at the time that I write this, one vital piece of research remains to be done, while my publishers have expressed their confidence and optimism from what they have seen of the early draft chapters. As my Literary Agent has helped me so much with research for my last book, not to mention her hundreds of hours of unpaid typing, am confident that she will, with help if necessary, bring my final project to a triumphant conclusion. Trusting that this will indeed happen, and with the agreement of my Trustees, I wish my Literary Agent to have a float for necessary travel and incidental expenses, and to receive all royalties earned by the book. My Literary Agent, who should be known to my solicitor, is Miss Melanie Mulligan.

As Pym looked up from his reading, there was a moment of total silence. Then Edward shot from his chair, emerging from the shadowed end of the table. "Let me see that!" He all but tore the paper out of the solicitor's grasp. Hand shaking, Edward read, forming some of the words through white lips. "But this is all written in layman's language!" He paused. "And the signature's not even witnessed! Pym, ought it not to have been witnessed?"

Looking very far from comfortable, Winston Pym regained possession of the paper. Turning to Kate he said, "Mr Upchurch is quite right. This declaration can be challenged on more than one ground. To be legally enforceable Mr Farley's signature should have been witnessed by an independent witness, and besides that what we have here is merely a photocopy and I have no idea where the original could be."

Edward stormed back to his seat. "Well I'll be damned if this Miss Mulligan sees a single penny. Apparently, Pym, you know her; well I can assure you, we know her too!"

Silent until this moment, Kate reached over for the paper. "This is definitely my husband's signature. I don't care about witnesses or any of that. We will observe Blane's wishes to the letter."

Ralph on Assignment

Wanting to experience New York's Manhattan Island, if only for 24 hours, Ralph Ransome made Kennedy his landfall. Emerging from the terminal he found yellow cabs and to spare. He took the first in line.

The cabman launched into conversation the moment the car was slammed into gear. After quick-fire exchanges about heat and humidity, Ralph was accosted with, "Say Pal, you been in Nam recently?" Ralph deduced he was being asked about Vietnam and America's ongoing war. He also guessed the patterns of his face had invited the question. Not eager to hear about "little yellow men" and the efficacy of Napalm, he responded with, "Oh, I'm just a Limey from over the Pond, and this was an accident." The cabby hit back with, "Well, Pal, I hope you gave the other guy as good as he gave you, yeah?"

After that Ralph's driver shut up, evidently sensing he was landed with a poor conversationalist. In place of the interrogation, the car's radio burst into rowdy life. It was the time of day for something called the "Dan Ingram Fringram," informing Ralph in between the Beach Boys and the Beatles that Eastern Parkway was closed for much of its length due to a major incident.

The next day Ralph boarded the Amtrack service out of New York City's Grand Central station, settling himself in a corner seat for the journey to Boston. For the umpteenth time he fingered his breast pocket, reassuring himself that the wallet containing the precious banker's draft was securely stowed away. This was his first time to cross the Atlantic. Ralph felt nervous, yet he also wanted to feel exhilarated.

The overnight flight from London's Heathrow had battled with fierce head-winds and had not been comfortable. He had slept little. As a result he found himself dozing, lulled by the rhythm of the pullman. Half in and out of consciousness he fancied at one point he was sharing the experience of those Old World emigrants so hauntingly re-imagined in the closing lines of Fitzgerald's epic roman-a-clef, fleeting glimpses of Dutch-style architecture feeding the notion. Musing on Gatsby, he wondered dimly, "Is there a future for Ralph Ransom, or am I merely one of those 'Boats against the current'?"

As the town of Springfield approached, Ralph sensed heightened activity all around him. The hawkers of roasted peanuts raised their game noisily while luggage was thrown down from the overhead racks. A rush of passengers boarding at Springfield were loud with their anticipation of the evening's game. Knowing nothing about America's national obsession, Ralph yet understood there was to be something called a "double-header" involving the Boston Red Socks, happening at a crucial point in the World Series. Men, women, children all around him could barely wait, it seemed, to get to their televisions to witness the clash of titans.

Stepping down from the train at South Boston, Ralph was not a little relieved to be met in person by his brother's named contact. The greeting was warm and welcoming. "Mr Ralph Ransom, Sir? Yes, here we are, Mason Greenhill at your service! Please, let me take that bag for you. Good journey, I hope?"

Ralph found he was looking up at the scholarly face of an extremely tall man, a rakishly cocked Derby adding to the impression of height. "I've got a cab waiting right along, and we'll have you sitting at Mrs Greenhill's dinner table in no time at all."

Mrs Greenhill's dining table proved as welcoming as Mrs Greenhill herself. Catharina Greenhill, it seemed, was descended from Swedish immigrant parents, while Mason, as he proudly confided, could trace his ancestry back some four generations, ultimately to County Sligo.

After a mountainous meal featuring the most succulent sea food Ralph had ever tasted, the men walked it off with a stroll around Old Boston, their way lit by antique gas mantles.

Next day and Ralph was being introduced to Mason's emporium of old books, hundreds even thousands of them. He pictured his brother's dusty stock, deciding it was very much the poor relation to the abundance he now feasted on. Tomes devoted to America's Civil War alone occupied half a dozen shelves. Ralph thought he had been told, presumably by Kate, that Blane Farley had been absorbed in the subject and had even embarked on research for a possible book. Ralph reached down a volume at random, a commentary on McClellan's Peninsular Campaign, and was reading with concentration when Mason came around to tap him lightly on the shoulder. "I sure am sorry to interrupt your studies, Ralph, but you see, today's Friday, so I would dearly like to get that money order into the bank."

"Why yes, of course, it's right here," patting his breast pocket. "No problem at all, but ..."

"Right, you're wondering, where is the merchandise? So, before you hand anything over, let me level with you. The prize possession you have come all this way to collect is not here in Boston, but in the very safe custody of my sister Grace, the real Dickinson devotee of the family. Grace lives an hour or two from here, and I can tell you, she is looking forward to meeting her first true Britisher. So then, the question is, do you trust me to take you out there to complete the deal having parted with the old spondoolicks?"

Ralph retreated half a step, brain whirring. This was not a contingency for which he had been briefed by brother Philip. The banker's draft ought to afford instant credit - that would certainly be the case back home - but did it work the same way with an American bank? It was quite possible, Ralph reasoned, that Mason needed to establish the worth of the payment before parting with such a valuable folio. Should he place a call to Philip to seek his instruction? No, he decided, that would look less than trusting, and he so badly wanted to trust the New Englander.

Ralph looked Mason squarely in his unblinking eye. The gaze held without the merest suspicion of double dealing. Ralph reached into his breast pocket and retrieved the envelope containing the draft.

....

Mason and Ralph had an easy journey out of Boston the following morning. They made good time to the State-line where Massachusetts became New Hampshire. Clapboarded homesteads dotted the landscape at random; lake and woodland sparkled on all sides. Here and there the green was tinged with gold. Was this, Ralph mused, the harbinger of the New England Fall, he had heard so much about?

"Let me put you in the picture concerning Grace," Mason edged his glance sideways towards his passenger. "She's a genuine one-off is my eccentric sister. Insists on living on her own in the middle of the woods, existing most of the time on the nuts and the mushrooms she harvests herself. Fine cook, mind you, besides a devoted disciple of Rachel Carson, the Conservationist, don't you know."

"While spending her time with the Bard of Amherst?" Ralph prompted.

"Oh boy! You bet! Reckon she has everything ever published, along with transcripts on to tape which she's always listening to when not deep in the short stories of Jorge Luis Borges, her other obsession."

"Listening? Do you mean? ..."

"Yes, Grace is blind, totally blind."

Some miles short of the State Capital of Concord, Mason slowed and they left the turnpike to bump down a gravel track that extended for several hundred yards. At the end of the track Ralph found he was looking at a wide-fronted single storey dwelling complete with pillared entrance and wraparound veranda. Clapboard painted in startling white lent the whole an air of prim security.

Waiting for them on the stoop, dressed in white from her Alice band down to her high-buttoned boots, stood Grace Greenhill. "Hi you all! Coffee's perking. Come along in."

Inhaling deeply the rich loamy tang of the woodland setting, Ralph mounted to the stoop, followed by Mason. Inside the house, before anything else happened, he was bidden, "Freshen up that away," courtesy of Grace's precisely pointed direction. He obeyed.

A few minutes later and he was sat down at the workaday piecrust table in Grace Greenhill's kitchen. Grace was serving out coffee. "Sure is good to be meeting you, Ralph! I badly want to hear all about you, and all about that England of yours; but before that you must see what you've come all this way for. Don't want you wondering if you've come on a wild goose chase, that right, Mason?"

Coffee mugs sided away to avoid any chance of accident, Grace conjured from some hidden place on her body the book for which Philip's client was paying so much money. As the book was laid flat on the table top, Ralph lent over to compare his brother's photographs with the original. As he had never doubted, the match was exact.

"Hey now! What an exquisite little item!"

Ralph's enthusiasm was unrestrained. "It's somehow, well, somehow smaller than I'd been expecting." He continued to pour over the script. "And the writing, so small and precise; are you telling me this is her writing, Miss Dickinson's own hand?"

"You bet it is," Grace's voice swelled with pride. "There's no date, sadly, but Mason and I worked out the collection must have been put together in her late teenage. Open it up, why don't you? Have a proper look through."

Ralph leafed through the folio with concentration. Somewhere in an adjoining room an American wall clock of ante-bellum vintage ticked busily on its way. Brother and sister Greenhill sat on in silence. Some of the pages of the little book, Ralph noticed, were badly foxed with spots of mildew; but Philip had warned him that this might well be the case, so he said nothing about it.

Sensing that their guest had come to the end of his examination, Grace broke the silence. "If you let me wrap Emily in tissue, I guess she will slip nice into that jacket pocket with no danger of her going astray over the ocean, yeah?"

Their business done, the three of them got to talking. Grace especially was keen to hear about those titles then popular on book lists around the universities of England, as well as the latest cult novels. Ralph told of his students' fad for reciting chunks of Joseph Heller's *Catch 22*, which struck no chords with Grace or her brother. With James Baldwin, Ralph sparked much greater interest. As for Borges, Grace did not hold back; she could not understand why the Argentinian essayist was not better known and regarded on either side of the Atlantic.

After two hours their coffee-fuelled debates finally faltered when Mason spied Ralph checking his watch. "Grace dear, we don't want that our friend grow tired of our chatter, start worrying about his travelling plans."

Grace responded, as if on cue. "Well, you boys must just stay over for a night. If you haven't brought anything with you, Ralph, Mason can surely fix you up. Always keeps spare pyjamas, tooth brush and so on right here with me."

They dined on nut cutlets. Ralph understood the nut cutlet was one of Grace's specialities. Politely he chomped his way through the experience, while the generous drafts of Mead, topped off by a fiery pear brandy greatly aided digestion. So it was that Ralph retired to his sleeping quarters in the warmth of alcohol and good fellowship, lapsing at once into deep sleep.

Sometime well after midnight, Ralph was disturbed. The skittering sound scratched at his brain, a sound quite alien. Eventually he worked it out. A creature of some kind was either on the roof or seeking for warmth from the flue. Might it, he wondered vaguely, be that half-tame scavenger, the "Johnny Chuck" mentioned in passing during the day?

Then there was something else. Turning in the bed, his back to the wall Ralph found he was no longer alone. Blinking through thin shards of moonlight spilling in through the latticed windows, he started with surprise. Lying next to him was Grace.

Sheathed in white, a blue ribbon nestling her pale neck, Grace was propped on an elbow, and seemed to be staring directly into Ralph's eyes. "I hope you will pardon me, Mr Englishman. Just had a yen to do this. Couldn't help myself."

Afraid his visitor might be in danger of slipping from the side of the bed, Ralph wriggled back an inch, drawing Grace towards him. "Please," he murmured, "That's all right."

"Mason told me you'd had an accident, a bad accident. You got yourself burned. Do I have that right?"

"You have that right."

"Would you mind terribly if I were to …?"

Ralph reached out for the girl's fingertips, guiding them gently to his face. With a slow delicacy she proceeded to trace the contours, one by one, the rough and the smooth. When she had finished she said with a soft breath, "Have tips to my fingers, can see. That's why I'm here, by the way, rudely waking you up, not to seduce, but to get near, perhaps to explain something."

Annoyingly, glimpses of Rita and instant gratification chased through his brain, his stomach, but flashed out again. Grace's rapt and gentle face held him. How much better than taking, was giving; how much better than giving, was sharing.

Ralph turned to Grace to ask, "Surely, you must be sad to be parting with your Emily?"

Her silence lasted so long he thought she had dropped back asleep. Eventually she said, "That is what I wanted to explain. I have no choice. I must have an operation, and this is the only way I'll get to pay for the surgery. But don't you worry, dear Ralph, Emily is tucked away safe in here," tapping her forehead, "And what matters even more than that is, we, you and I, we have shared precious time together."

Edward Makes an Offer

Edward wanted to drive Kate back to Deering before returning north. He had a lot he was burning to say to his sister. Not wanting to be on the receiving end of a diatribe, even fearing that in Edward's wrought-up state he might cause an accident, Kate made the excuse that she had urgent shopping to do at the Army & Navy, and managed to slip away from Winston Pym's office without further confrontation. If she got her timing right, Kate thought she might just catch Melanie returning home from work. Edward protested of course, but was left staring at his sister's back until the throngs of High Holborn swallowed her up.

As he wove and jostled his way out of the City and up to the motorway midst much honking and gesturing towards uncooperative fellow travellers, Edward stewed over events. The whole Blane thing rankled, challenging his instinct for what was proper, what was decent, even what was heroic. For Edward had always had a passion for what he could not have in his own life, the heroism of others. Even as the first German bombs were falling on Sheffield, some twenty miles from his High Peaks home, Edward had been given to burying himself under his bed clothes, pocket torch in hand, to wrap himself in high-flown accounts of daring-do from the rich tapestry of colonial history.

Edward's favourite hero was General Gordon of Khartoum.

Blissfully unaware of any charge of quixotry that might later be applied to the General, Edward knew only that his hero had stood alone against the dastardly Mahdi. The picture of the flying spear that was said to have felled Gordon was the emblem most cherished by the six-year-old. On every rereading of the epic story he was unable to sleep until he had revisited the battle of Omdurman, for the reassurance that Gordon's sacred sacrifice had been avenged by those magnificent Redcoats.

Less venerated than General Gordon but much nearer to his Edward's own age, Ensign Piccard shone as bright as any hero after nearly 200 years. An employee of the British East India Company, Piccard had held off the attackers of Fort William in Bengal, to be the last man standing after a small but fierce engagement. Tragically Piccard was finally captured, to be entombed in the infamous Black Hole of Calcutta where he was amongst those who had suffocated to death. But then, in short order, Robert Clive had arrived to trounce "the natives" at the battle of Plassey.

Denied the role of the hero in his own rather more pedestrian life, Edward was yet able to fall back on two constants, two most trustworthy lines in the sand. The first of these was his profession of Chartered Accountant and his membership of the Institute. The key, of course, was numbers. Numbers did not lie; numbers never failed to repay the trust that you put in them. If a page of numbers failed to add up, there was always a logical reason which Edward with his quick forensic eye was invariably able to fathom.

For Edward was a man who dealt in facts. Facts were all that mattered in life. If he had time to read at all, it was to his professional magazines with their statistical analyses that he turned, for he had no time for fiction. Had he ever discovered the works of Charles Dickens, it would have been Mr Gradgrind to whom he would have related. The boringly drawn-out adventures and misadventures of Nicholas Nickleby not to mention Pip's "great expectations," would have left him cold.

It followed therefore that Edward avoided speculation like the plague. Speculation was the enemy of fact. This went to explain why he had never got on with Ralph. Ralph loved nothing more, it seemed to Edward, than to while away a whole evening speculating with anyone who would listen, about famous turning points in history. Edward had once been on the fringes of a debate lasting several hours, devoted entirely to the battle of Waterloo. Ralph had posed the question, "What do we think would have happened had Napoleon Bonaparte launched his attack two hours earlier while Field Martial Blucher and his Prussians were still 13 miles distant from the field?" Edward had muttered an excuse and slunk away. Wellington had won the battle - Fact! That was all that mattered, apart possibly from analysis of the troop numbers engaged on either side.

The second constant in Edward's life was his Lodge. Edward had been a Freemason for ten years and more and had recently gone through the Chair of his Lodge as the youngest Worshipful Master for decades.

There were two things about Masonry that appealed to Edward above all others. He loved the precision and the predictability of the ritual that inspired trust in much the same way that numbers inspired trust. He admired the benevolent core of the order; but most of all he related to the old fashioned civility of the Brethren. No meeting of the Lodge would pass by without the fraternal round of handshakes and enquiries as to one's health. And then again, there was the Masons' time-honoured regard for widows and orphans, a further reason - if Edward needed it - for despising his brother-in-law, the waster and adulterer. Yes, Edward mused, as the Daimler swept off the motorway at Junction 25, he really must do something about his misguided sister and the pickle that Blane had left behind.

....

So it was that Edward Upchurch stood outside Melanie Mulligan's flat one Sunday morning. On his way south Edward had called in on his sister, sneaking a look at her address book while Kate was busy chopping onions.

Melanie answered the door in her dressing gown. There was no single person she could have expected to come calling at eleven o'clock on a Sunday morning, so that her face still wore the pallor of the night, freckles standing out in relief, while her feet were bear.

"How do you do? My name is Upchurch, Edward Upchurch. Kate Farley is my sister. Do you think I might come in for a minute of your time?"

Melanie stared at her visitor. Even then she had a premonition that this dapperly dressed man would have nothing good to say to her. All the same, she removed the chain from the door and beckoned Edward in.

"I'm afraid you will have to excuse the mess. I wasn't really up when you knocked." She indicated a chair for her guest to sit down.

Edward opted not to sit, preferring instead to look out of the window. "Fine view you have here, Miss ..."

"My name is Mulligan, Melanie Mulligan. Are you going to tell me what you want?"

After some further moments of river watching, Edward turned back to face the girl. "No my dear, it's not a case of what I want, rather more a case of what you will be wanting." As he spoke, Edward retrieved a chequebook from his briefcase, together with a Parker pen from which he unscrewed the top.

Melanie collapsed down on to the sofa. "I'm sorry, but I have no idea what you mean."

Edward opened the chequebook, laying it flat on the windowsill. "I'm asking you to name your price. How much money do you want?"

"I don't understand, and I don't want any money." Melanie lowered her head to her hands. Already she knew or thought she knew what this was about.

Edward levered himself away from the window with the gesture of impatience. "Come, come! Mrs Farley has obviously told you about my brother-in-law's, hmm, wishes, book royalties and so forth. Not to mince words, I'm here to pay you off. I give you a cheque; you bank that cheque, and by doing so you sever all connection with Blane Farley and his family. So then, shall we settle on, say, £500?"

The taut smile that momentarily creased Edward's smooth features meant that he was utterly unprepared for the girl's reaction. With a reflex bound Melanie shot from the sofa, hands pushing out in front of her face in a gesture of blind rage. "Out! Get out of my flat! Now!"

Edward barely had time to pouch pen and chequebook before finding himself outside the girl's front door. Any crumb of doubt as to the outcome of his visit was loudly removed by the slamming shut of the door behind him.

Invitation to the Ball

Tudors was old, though not nearly as old as its name would suggest. The original house, planted solidly on a rising swell of land facing south and west, dated from the early years of Victoria's reign, owing its construction to one Lancelot Tudor. Through ties of blood, the house had come into the ownership of the Ransom family who had added considerably to its footprint over the years.

A particular trigger for the expansion had come in the early years of the new century around the time that the ageing Prince of Wales was wheezing his way to the throne. This was in the time of Sir Hector's father, and followed a serious fire. Attributed to spite on the part of a disaffected footman, this fire had gutted the east wing while making inroads on the finely appointed ballroom on the farther side of the house. Having inherited Tudors and its acres, escaping lightly on death duties, Hector's father, Francis, had used a growing fortune from shipping to build out to the east, adding a number of bedrooms and renovating the ballroom in style, the feature, an elegant semi-circular gallery.

Despite his investment, Francis Ransom had spent little time at Tudors, preferring to divide his time between the French Riviera and the City of London and its levers of finance. Hardly a step had he strutted in his proud ballroom. His eldest son was a different matter. Hector aspired to social status. Including prestigious roles as Master of Foxhounds and chairmanship of his local bench of magistrates, he bestrode the county as a man of moment, raising vast sums for charity, in his home county and further afield.

In these endeavours Hector was greatly aided by two things. The first of these was his war record. Active in the ranks of the local Yeomanry from an early age, he had proved an energetic recruiter of men once the German Kaiser had sent his grey hordes flooding into "Little Belgium." Some way into the war, his commission came through, and soon, due to the drain of baton-wielding officers, he found he was commanding a battalion. The Third Battle of Ypres launched in rivers of mud, with Hector surviving unscathed. Then in the March the following year the great enemy offensive rolled down over the battlefields of earlier in the war, threatening to pin the allied armies to the sea. Hector with the remnants of his command had been cut off and all but surrounded. Hector had been wounded in the leg and shipped back to hospital in England, his war ended. Yet Hector's wound had not proved life-threatening. Discharged from the hospital after a mere three weeks, he walked with a palpable limp, though this was to prove little hindrance to his burgeoning progress as one of the county's leaders. Some less charitable wags hinted that the limp was exaggerated; while all who knew him agreed that "Hector Ransom had enjoyed a Good War."

The second great aid was Beatrice. For years after the war, Hector had been content to play the field where girls were concerned. Dalliances came and went while Hector devoted much of his energies to fox hunting and, came the General Strike, the driving of railway engines. Then one January night, the night of the Hunt Ball, Beatrice burst into his life.

Beatrice Campbell was a child of The Ascendancy, her grandparents originating from England and from Scotland. Her father was a surgeon at Belfast's leading hospital, specialising in the treatment of burns. Her mother, between raising a large family, was coordinator of the local Waifs and Strays Society. "All," as they said at the time, "was as it should be" with the Campbells, but for one thing. Beatrice's mother had been born and raised a Catholic. This was a secret that her mother had largely suppressed, while yet succeeding in planting the precious seed into the heart of young Beatrice.

At the Hunt Ball, hosted with elaborate attention to detail at Tudors, Beatrice, then undergoing nurse's training at one of London's famous teaching hospitals, made a beeline for Hector, scattering bevies of young debs and their mothers in the process. Hector was smitten. The couple were married in six months, Beatrice's only stipulation being their children be raised in the Catholic Faith.

Over the years that followed the children had been born with commendable regularity, Ralph and Philip being followed by their sisters. Hector had been knighted for services to his community and to charity. If some people unfamiliar with the mysteries of the Honours system imagined that the local squire had somehow inherited his title, Lady Ransom did not disabuse them. Others whispered among themselves that the honour was down to Beatrice's friendship with a Catholic Peer; Beatrice disdained to hear the whispers. Finally, after the running to earth of many a fox, there had come that New Year's Day, scintillating with frost, when the dying Sir Hector had been brought in from the field, just minutes after a view.

Now Beatrice sat at her escritoire, leafing through her address book. It was Tudors' turn to host the annual charity ball, and besides putting on a good show, Beatrice was determined to take advantage of the occasion to get the family together and, more pointedly, to match-make. For Beatrice had not given up on the business of finding a wife for her eldest son. The Ransom line, after all, depended on it.

Beatrice did not underestimate the task. While she was in denial as to the graphic impact of Ralph's injuries, she was yet canny enough to realise that his chances of shining in their social circles were diminished. Somehow - Beatrice suspected their gardener Dent - word had got out. Following a committee meeting of Children's League of Pity, Mandy Brakespeare had taken Beatrice aside to ask in the loudest of whispers, "So sorry to hear about young Ralph. I suppose its dark rooms and buckets of sympathy from now on?" And this would have been water off the proverbial duck's back, but for the fact that Mandy Brakespeare was a rival to Beatrice in the hostess stakes.

The trawl of her address book proved depressingly unrewarding. Many a promising lead crashed up against one buffer or another, reminding Beatrice of her son's obduracy at their last meeting. With a theatrical sigh she slammed the book down and was about to put off the planning of the best social event of the Season when, not one but, two inspirations hit her in quick succession.

....

It had taken Melanie days to get over the visit from Edward Upchurch. The anger still burned in her. What right had this self-important little man to cheapen Blane's memory, and why on earth should he assume she was willing to be bought? But then, between the sustaining anger, there crept in odd moments of doubt and introspection. Had she led Blane on? Should she have run away as soon as she tumbled to the truth about his wife and family? Had she amended the pattern of her young life and gone to confession back then, she had little doubt what the priest would have said, what the priest would have instructed.

Then there was something else that weighed on Melanie's mind. Kate had been perfectly sweet about the trust thing, handing over a copy of Blane's wishes, making it clear that she would not stand in the girl's way when it came to completion and publication of the book. The problem was, Melanie really had no idea where or how to start. She knew perfectly well what Blane had been aiming at, yet she was not Blane. She tried desperately to summon

Blane to her, pretending he was lying in bed beside her. She pictured his eyes; she strained to hear his voice; it was no good; she was stuck, "held in suspended animation," to quote a phrase she had once read. Then, out of the blue, a letter dropped into her box.

Written in a strong hand on headed notepaper, the letter read:-

Dear Miss Melanie Brannigan,

When you tracked us down at Tudors back in the Summer, you may remember I promised to let you know when my son Ralph would be visiting next. So, I am glad to say that I expect him here next month, the occasion our annual Charity Ball, which Tudors is hosting this year.

I very much hope, my dear, you will feel like killing two birds, so to speak, by delivering that message to Ralph in person while enjoying a jolly time at the dance.

As you will see from the enclosed invitation, I and my Committee have decided on a masked ball, as this has not been done for a few years now. Oh, and I hope you will forgive me for also enclosing a little something for travel.

You will see our telephone number at the top of this letter. Do please give me a tinkle, and do please tell me that you will be free to join us.

The letter was signed with a flourish and ended with a postscript. "Bye the bye, please don't worry about getting back to town after the Ball. Tudors has beds and to spare."

....

Tudors was en fete. The great house vibrated from end to end with a shrill of young voices competing in volume with the Quicksteps, the Polkas and Viennese Waltzes being served up by the live band. Holly and mistletoe overflowed the sconces lining the walls; everywhere a sweet melange of that year's perfumes spiced the air.

The Ball was already in full swing when Melanie got out of her taxi and, not without a frisson, tripped up the steps to the front door. Not sure whether she should already be masked, she clutched the home-made item so as to show that it was ready for wearing. As it turned out, this proved the right thing to do. Relieved of her coat by a uniformed young man, she found she had no time to take a breath, as immediately she was shaking hands with Beatrice herself. "Dear Gal, I am so pleased you have come. Welcome to Tudors! Now I'm afraid that wretched boy of mine has yet to put in an appearance, but he will. And meantime there are lots of lovely people who I know will be delighted to meet you. Delicious dress, by the way! Midnight blue, am I right?"

Masked, Melanie braved the dance. To begin with, she found it unnerving. She knew nobody. Telling the men from the women was no problem, yet discerning the age behind the mask, let alone the features, was quite impossible. Viewing the garish varieties of masks was at least a pleasant distraction, as was supper where her hostess joined Melanie, whispering that Ralph had at last been sighted. "Can always spot him by his awful red socks!" Beatrice explained.

Following Dashing White Sergeant and Strip-the-willow, the next up after supper was a Barn-dance in which the men circled a phalanx of ladies. Whenever the band stopped playing, each man stepped forward to claim an individual dance with the girl opposite to him.

Lent over the gallery balustrade, Beatrice was able to catch the eye of the band leader, who had been tipped off to expect her signal. As Ralph drew opposite Melanie, Beatrice dropped her lace handkerchief and the music subsided in the middle of a bar. Dancers shimmied into couples and the band struck up again, this time with a Waltz taking the dancers once around the floor before the music stopped a second time, the band leader announcing, "This, Ladies and Gentlemen, is the Statue Dance!"

Each time the music stopped the dancers were expected to freeze in mid-step. Couples were eliminated and had to leave the floor if they or either of them moved a muscle before the music picked up. There was something mildly erotic about the whole thing as dancers often found they were clutching previously unexplored body parts or clinging to each other for balance. Ralph and Melanie, Beatrice noticed with satisfaction, were each revelling in the other's company and doing a lot of clinging. They might even, she thought, end up as prize winners, the last couple standing.

Carriages had been ordered for two in the morning, so around half passed the hour, following repeated drum rolls, a hullabaloo of departing guests rippled and echoed through the house. Bursts of high spirits bounced back and forth; a glass or two crashed on to stone; a hunting horn brayed a valedictory blast.

By this time a very happy Melanie was seated on a sofa in Ralph's first floor sitting room, a glass of Pimms - at least her third of the evening - close to hand. "You look as if you're still in the dance, Master Ralph. Aren't you going to sit down?" This with a pat of the sofa.

Still restless, Ralph poured himself a drink before coming to perch alongside Melanie. "Well, the Ma will be pleased; ticket sales must have been huge this time around."

Guilt clouded Melanie's face. "Oh heavens! I didn't realise. Should I have bought a ticket?"

"Totally not. Ma was on a mission when she invited you along. I hope you don't mind?"

"I'd mind less if you came and shared this comfy sofa with me."

Ralph obeyed, stretching long legs out in front of him. "Thanks for the message from dear old Blane, by the way. You and he, you were, hmm, friends?"

Melanie lowered her head. Downstairs a last door slammed shut. In a small voice she replied, "Yes we were, we were friends." A silence, and then, "I think I may have seen you at Blane's funeral that day?"

"I was there, at least in spirit. How? ..."

"How did I know? Okay, so that doesn't matter. I'm sorry, let's not talk about funerals. I just want you to know how much I've enjoyed tonight. But I do wish you would let me see your face, your eyes, properly I mean. Haven't you had that silly mask on long enough? Mine came off ages ago in case you hadn't noticed!"

"Oh you bet, I noticed all right." Ralph reached a hand across the gap between their bodies. For long moments he gazed into her face, looking only at the dancing eyes.

Impulse overtook Melanie. Laughter on her lips she reached up and deftly released the elastic ties from around Ralph's ears. The mask slid down the dress shirt, to tumble end over end across the floor.

The naked moment seemed to last for ever. The girl shrank away. Then she was on her feet and groping for the door. "Oh God no, I'm sorry, but I can't do this."

Cerys

Ralph raced through the remainder of the night. He drove fast because there was someone he was desperate to see, to connect with.

Ralph pulled into the hospital car park as dawn was creeping up over the roof tops. Without bothering to lock the car, or even close his door, he ran up the steps and burst into Reception. "I need to see Deaconess Hunter."

The middle-aged woman at the desk looked up, a frown already pasted on her end-of-the-shift face. "Sorry, who are you asking for?"

"Your Almoner, Deaconess Hunter, Cerys Hunter."

With a small shrug of reluctance the woman consulted a roster. "It would seem Miss Hunter is on annual leave as from Friday of last week."

"So can you give me her address or her telephone number?"

The woman bristled visibly. "Oh no, certainly not. We're not allowed to give out personal details of that sort. You really should have made an appointment, assuming you are a patient here." And she slotted the roster back in its cubbyhole.

For several seconds Ralph stood on the spot, rage and frustration competing to take control. Then he turned on his heel and left the hospital. From the hospital Ralph drove a mile to the city centre where he found a cafe just then opening for business. The girl on duty sounded anything but English, so Ralph simply pointed to the first item on the menu, not really concerned as to what he was ordering.

The food arrived with suspicious speed. He ate a mouthful, but left the rest to congeal on the plate. The coffee though was good, and he asked for a re-fill.

Outside again and the city was coming alive, though reluctantly, the dregs of Saturday night still on its breath. Ralph decided on a stiff walk to see if it would clear his head.

As he strode the anonymous streets, one after another, Ralph tried to picture his face the last time he had peered into that implacable mirror. Back then, before the Ball - was it only hours ago? - he had thought his face was improving. The girl had told him a different story. Restlessly roaming the house he had ticked off a very short list of people he might talk to. His mother was not on the list. Philip was no good; Philip would only wheel out comparisons with figures of fiction. Edward was no good; Edward would only treat with scorn and "I told you so!" Then of course there was Kate.

Kate would sit down with him, take his hand, and listen to him; yet the outcome was sure to be pity. The idea of Miss Hunter had come to him in a flash. With her calm face, her steady gaze, Miss Hunter was bound to understand, bound to bring perspective … But Miss Hunter was not there.

Ralph automatically turned a corner and almost immediately fell sprawling to the pavement. Staggering to his feet he registered two things. He saw that what had tripped him up was a pair of legs protruding from a shop doorway. The other thing he realised as he began to brush himself down was his suit, the very same dress suit he had worn for the ball and which, in his haste and confusion, he had not thought about changing.

"Gawd almighty! We've got a right flunky here! Can't you look where you're going, Mate?"

"Gosh! I'm terribly sorry. Didn't see your, hmm, feet there." Ralph peered down at the face evidently belonging to the feet. "Can I help? Have you had an accident at all?"

Henry, for it turned out that was the man's name, unfurled himself from layers of cardboard and newspaper to prop himself onto an elbow. "Yes Mate, as it happens, you can, help I means. You can call me Henery by the way." "Henery" came out with an exaggerated haitch.

"So what can I do for you?"

"You can wet me whistle, that's what you can do for me. Bloomin' perishing kipping here all night it is."

"So it's a coffee is it?"

"No Mate, it ain't coffee, more like a tot or two of the hard stuff." And Henry, finger in mouth, launched a piercing whistle on the morning air.

Almost at once as it seemed, a scruffy ossity of a lad barely in his teens, lurched around the corner, eyeing Ralph with blatant curiosity. "Right now young Jason, this 'er genleman is keen to buy Henry a little drink, so bugger off and get my usual, quick-sticks, yeah?"

Ralph tried his pockets one by one, to check that his wallet was still in the jacket of his suit. "I'm afraid I've only got a fiver. Will that do?"

"Champion, Mr Genleman, champion." The boy Jason grabbed the note and raced off. "I do like your snazzy glad rags. Fancy selling?"

"Well actually no. You see …"

"'Cause if you does, I knows a punter round the corner who'll give you a good price, and kit you out with something in return." This with a discordant riff on Henry's Mouth Organ by way of punctuation.

....

"Melanie!" Cerys Hunter flung the door wide as the girl fell into her arms. "All right, all right, come on dear. Easy, easy." She half led, half carried the girl to the sofa. "Has something happened to you? You haven't had an accident, have you?"

Melanie sank on the sofa, her head in her hands, hot tears squeezing between her fingers.

After a long silence during which Cerys sat calmly watching her surprise visitor, Melanie finally looked up. "No, I haven't had an accident, not in the way you mean."

"Well, that's something at least." Cerys got up, going to the kitchen to put the kettle on. Over her shoulder she added, "No rush, Dear, I'm not working today, so you've got me all to yourself."

The tea made, Cerys resumed her seat opposite to Melanie. "I hope I've remembered how you like your tea? As I say, there's no possible rush; just say when you're ready to talk."

For moments Melanie stared at Cerys, her tea cradled between shaking hands. "Last night - God, was it only last night - I had a wonderful time, a really wonderful time at a dance, a Hunt Ball where everyone wore masks. By chance or not - doesn't really matter - I met this really nice guy. He was, he is, hmm older than me, but we talked and talked and danced of course. It was obvious that he'd been around, found his own world, if you know what I mean. Yet he didn't talk down to me, and he listened, he actually listened to me and my chatter."

To bring a long pause to an end, Cerys asked, "So do you want to tell me what happened once the dancing stopped?"

"He, his name is Ralph, Ralph took me up to his sitting room. I didn't know what I was expecting, but I was so happy I just wanted things to go wherever they might go." And after a gulp of tea, "It was obvious we couldn't relax with our masks still on, so I took mine off. He seemed reluctant to take his off, so I did the worst possible thing, I did it for him, and ..."

"And you found a strange, a haunted face bursting through your happiness, and you panicked. Is that right?"

Melanie dashed her teacup down and half rose from the sofa. "Yes, but how? ..."

"Did I know? Let's just say I put two and two together, and leave it at that. Yes?"

"Since that terrible moment I've been thinking back to the last time we talked. Remember, you told me about the rainbow; you told me that each of us has one precious thing inside us; you taught me that God has placed us above the animals by giving us the gift of empathy." She slumped back to the cushions. "So now I suppose you'll tell me I owe it to God to forget what has happened to me, and to carry on as if nothing happened last night?"

Cerys fingered the small cross at her neck. "No, I'm not going to tell you anything of the sort. I'm going to challenge you to a game of squash instead."

"Sorry, you're going to do what?"

"What you need is some good healthy and slightly violent exercise. Just so happens I have a court booked this morning at the university squash courts. I usually take my chance on finding an opponent, but today I've got you - and spare kit and sports bag, of course."

They set out. Melanie was not surprised they were walking to the university. For some reason it was not easy to picture Cerys behind the wheel of a car, and even had she owned such a thing she would have preferred to walk.

The streets near the centre were cloaked in Sunday silence. Then, as they turned a corner, the silence was abruptly shattered. A man dressed in raggedly shirt and trousers was propped against a wall, a mask of fear and bewilderment distorting the livid face. Squaring up to the man, two youths were taking it in turns to swing punches. One of the youths bizarrely was dressed in dinner jacket and trousers.

Melanie was the first to react to the desperate tableau. With the force of one possessed, she launched the heavy bag at the head of the first assailant so that he cannoned into his comrade, knocking them both off balance. As one, the women stepped in between Ralph and his persecutors who tried to face the women down before slinking away to cover.

Melanie turned back to Ralph. With deliberate care she reached up to cup his face in her hands, and to kiss his mouth.